LOOKING FOR CLARA

A NOVEL

SIMONA GROSSI

PIPES & CLOUDS

This book is a work of fiction. The characters, incidents, and dialogue are drawn from the author's imagination and are not to be construed as real. Any resemblances to actual events or persons, living or dead, is entirely coincidental.

Cover Design by Hazel Lam

Author Photo by Marco Paonessa

First Printing

ISBN: 1542439272

ISBN-13: 978-1542439275

To Mario

1

William is getting married tomorrow and I'm back in L.A. I've been away for over a year, and now everything looks like a stranger to me, even myself.

I wander through my apartment, run my fingers along the walls. Some of my trophies, the ones I collected before leaving, are still here, on my kitchen table. I remember assembling them and trying to decide whether I should take them with me. Wisely, I didn't.

A never-worn ring one of my relatives gave me when I graduated from law school. Precious, fancy. But too big for my fingers. Any of them. And I don't wear jewelry.

And that binder filled with documents I never read.... It belongs to my law firm. Ex law firm. I "won" the binder because I did well on another file. "You win this, Clara," my boss told me before leaving. Well, I did, and never worked on it.

And my Prada shoes. Here's one, damaged. I can barely see the "37" imprinted on its sole. I was supposed to take it to repair but never did. There was no time. Or will. I can still see myself wearing those heels and my black suit, checking myself in the mirror before a meeting, and trying to look exactly what I am not. A lawyer.

My memories are so loud they're taking over the entire apartment, me. I squeeze my eyes to impose some order on them, to make sense of them, but my headache is too strong, and the L.A. sun is so bright it almost hurts.

I feel like I came from a long swim underwater with my eyes open. I found my life and myself submerged. My eyes need to rest.

I pull the shades tightly, and drift into a trance where I can see more clearly how I got here.

2

I'm not sure why I went to law school. I had studied piano since almost before I can remember and then I stopped. The story I used to repeat, the one I gave anyone who asked, was that I couldn't play in public. But the truth was more complicated than that.

I stopped playing after college, spent the following two years doing next to nothing, and then applied to law school. I don't remember exactly how I formed that idea. Maybe it was a movie I saw, my father's vision for me, my need to become more assertive, or something else. It wasn't passion, though. I applied and got in.

My law school was in a dreary town in Connecticut, but the school was thought to be the top in the country. My classmates were young and absorbed in themselves. Although I guess I was too. I made very few friends, and was mainly alone.

I remember afternoons spent at my desk, my books open, staring at the snow and losing focus. Éric Satie was probably still playing in the back of my mind, but I had pressed it so far back I could barely hear it. And I kept sketching music notes on the margins of the Wright and Miller treatise, hoping its words would become more enticing at some point. My notes seemed suspended nowhere, and I was too.

The logic of law seemed much like the logic of music and I quickly took to that. I read and listened and absorbed. I would not participate in class, except when called on. I was mostly silent, certainly not a player on the law-school stage. And yet I graduated in the top 5% of the class. How did that happen? When I collected my degree, I still wasn't sure.

A few months later, I was offered and accepted a job at one of the top law firms in Los Angeles.

My parents were so happy when I gave them the news. They bought this apartment for me almost sight unseen. They probably thought it would be a good investment, the place where I would settle. I wanted to believe that too, but the unpacked boxes on my bedroom floor show that we were wrong. All of us were.

Life at the law firm was intense. Long days, late nights, lost weekends. The time was slipping through my fingers like sand in an hourglass I had turned upside down too quickly. And sometimes, when I paused to think about it, I almost missed the rootless two years after college, when not much was happening around me and I was just thinking and observing. At least, at that time, I had a sense of myself, something I seemed to have lost along the way.

I was committed to my work, and felt I should do my best to succeed. I had given up on music, and I didn't want to do the same with law. Maybe, if I didn't give up, I would feel happy. At some point. So I never said "no" to any of my colleagues, even when that meant piling more hours on top of more than I ever imagined possible. Sometimes I felt my office was my home. But I wasn't attached to it either. I just happened to spend more time there than anywhere else.

My colleagues were obsessed with their career trajectories, constantly trying to impress this or that partner, complaining about work with one breath and bragging about their long hours with another. For me, work was work. I wasn't planning any career or future with the law firm. I just happened to be there. I was attracted by the discipline, and I loved arguing, negotiating, and obviously winning. But I never paused to understand what was it about that job that I really liked. The essence of it, I mean. And it wasn't clear to me what exactly I was pursuing. Money for my client? Its victory? Mine?

I had no friends at the law firm, but I had a good relationship with Adam, my boss. I respected him and he trusted me. He was mostly honest, but he also knew how to play the game, and sometimes he would choose the game over me. I was so disappointed when that happened, but I forgave him. Yes, I did. Almost always. After all, law was the game we happened to be playing. He was a partner at a big law firm so he had played well. And maybe there wasn't any other way.

I worked hard, and would not filter my ideas if I believed in them. I would defend them against anyone, including those with more years and experience than me. Adam loved my ideas and dedication, but he didn't like my attitude. I thought he should be braver. He thought I should be *diplomatic* and *social* if I wanted to make it to partnership. I wasn't interested in that though, and I remained straightforward and somewhat aloof from my colleagues.

I would always try to avoid law firm parties, especially the Christmas ones. I hated those. They could make me feel even lonelier than I normally was.

So on Christmas Eve two years ago, when one of my colleagues asked me if I was coming to the firm's annual party, I knew I would not. I had just not made up an excuse yet. I had been busy on a file and had almost forgotten it was Christmas.

And then Adam came into my room to ask me whether I would join them. I thought he was referring to a meeting or a conference call. I said "sure" without even thinking, but when I asked him about the topic, he laughed and said, "Smith, you're really working too hard. You should get an extra drink tonight."

Right. The Christmas party. I wanted to say that I couldn't go, that I was too busy, but I knew he wouldn't buy it now, and the thought of another of his lectures on life at the law firm made me sick. So I remained silent, and swallowed my escape attempts. One by one.

On the short drive home from work, I looked outside the car's window. It really didn't feel like Christmas. I wasn't with my family. The streets were not covered in snow. The radio was not playing Christmas songs, and I was not waiting for any particular gift or surprise under the Christmas tree. In fact, I didn't even have a Christmas tree, unless you counted the small porcelain one the firm gave all the associates and employees. Still, it was Christmas, L.A. style. A scattering of twinkling lights, a Santa with sunglasses, fake snow sprayed on fake lawns, and traffic.

When I got home, I poured a glass of wine and listened to Debussy's *Arabesque No. 1*. I missed home and I missed William. We hadn't spoken in years. And yet, each Christmas, he would text me his holiday wishes, his own way. Not this year, though.

I poured more wine and entered the warm water of my bath, then my black dress, then my Prada shoes. I pushed some red lipstick onto my lips, forced a smile to check my teeth, checked the phone again, and called a taxi.

The streets of L.A. were now more crowded than they had seemed before. Everyone seemed headed to a party. The air was crisp with excitement. I was exhausted. I closed my eyes and fell into my own void. Suspended again, but unable to fly.

I sank more into the back seat, and looked at my shoes. They were uncomfortable, and one of them was slightly damaged. I looked at them and felt sad. That night I'd have rather been bare foot and walked free in my apartment. But I had to go to that party, and so I needed those shoes for my role. And I would play it well. A few more hours, and I'd be free.

When I arrived at the hotel, I paid the driver, and slipped out of the car. There was a loud sign near the entrance pointing toward a ballroom. I looked around. Women were wearing shiny black and gold dresses, extremely long or extremely short. And men were wearing tuxedos. They all seemed to be moving and talking too fast. I knew I would not be able to keep up with them. I couldn't. I was beyond tired from too many long days and nights and hadn't eaten since breakfast. So I guess the wine I had before kicked in more, and more quickly than anticipated. I tripped over something, lost balance, and fell.

"Are you O.K.?"

I looked up and saw a man in his late thirties, offering me his hand. He wasn't wearing a tuxedo. His suit was black, nice, perhaps a little too big for him.

"Yes. Thanks."

I took his hand as he helped me to my feet. I inspected my dress, brushed myself off, and walked toward the party. He followed me.

"Here for the party?" he asked.

"Yes." I looked at him and didn't recognize him from the firm, but maybe he was a new hire.

"You're a lawyer?" he asked, somewhat skeptically, I thought.

"Yes, I'm a lawyer." I kept walking, hoping he would leave me alone, but I was too slow.

"Aren't you a little short for a lawyer?"

"What?"

He laughed, "Sorry. Dumb joke," then stuck out his hand and said, "Hi. I'm Joe, a friend of Adam Sterling."

"Clara Smith," I said, and shook his hand as we walked together into the ballroom.

Were they truly friends? I couldn't see that. Adam was disciplined, almost military, and in fanatically good shape. Always impeccably dressed. This man was none of those things. He clearly didn't follow an exercise routine. He was a little soft around the edges, his hair had a mind of its own, thick and out-of-control, and his red flecked beard was anything but military. And though he wasn't "too short" to be a lawyer, he certainly didn't look like one.

"So this is the price you pay for being a lawyer, huh?" he said, indicating the noisy crowd that filled the room. "Do you like this sort of thing?"

I looked at him.

"Firm parties, I mean."

I looked around and did not respond. Of course I didn't like it.

As we stepped into the ballroom, Adam walked toward us.

"Do you know each other?" he asked.

"Yes," he said, but I said "No," and they laughed.

"We just met," Joe said, looking at me.

"Right," I said, and asked them to excuse me. I needed to find something to eat or else I would collapse.

There was a long buffet along the back wall and food stations throughout the room with every possible option, even a small sushi bar. I'd never thought of sushi as an option for a Christmas meal, so I ended up having that.

Christmas in L.A., I thought, and somehow surrendered to it, or became too tired to keep resisting.

I placed some sushi on my plate and walked to a couch where a few colleagues were gossiping about someone I didn't know. I asked if I could join them, but I actually didn't mean it. I just needed a place to sit and eat, a place where I could melt into the background and disappear.

"Absolutely," one of them said, Mark or Frank, I wasn't sure. They scooted over to make room for me, we exchanged smiles, and they returned to their gossip as if I were a pillow on the seat next to them.

The sushi was OK. I thought I should stay until I finished my meal and then leave, but then Joe returned.

"Sake?"

I looked up and saw him standing over me.

"That would be nice," I said, "but I don't think there is any."

"What about a glass of Chardonnay?"

I should have said no as I had drunk enough already, but I said yes, and he soon came back with two glasses. He handed me one and we toasted.

"To new friends," he said.

"To new friends," I echoed.

Yes, I had surrendered. It was probably the wine.

"You look bored."

"Maybe. Or maybe I'm over tired."

"They work you to death, right?"

"Sort of." I looked at him, and thought it would be nice to take off my shoes, walk out the door, and sit on the steps in the alley next to each other to chat about nothing. He didn't look like a lawyer.

"You're not a lawyer, right?"

He laughed.

"Me? No. Not for me. I'm a musician. Mostly jazz."

I raised my eyes from my plate to check him again and try to figure him out, but I may have stared at him for a little too long.

"Did I say something wrong?"

"No, I just love jazz."

"I knew you were too short to be a lawyer. What do you like?"

Were we chatting about nothing? There was still too much noise around, and it was hard to see things clearly.

"Debussy, Ravel, Miles Davis, Armstrong, Pink Floyd."

"You love music."

"I do," I confessed, and felt good about what I had just said.

He remained silent for a while, studying my hands as I took the last piece of sushi. Then Adam called him, and he excused himself.

I wandered around the ballroom, weaving around couples and groups. I thought it was interesting to see a looser version of my colleagues at play. They seemed different persons. I wondered how they could change so much when they were at work. Did I do the same?

I remained seated, immersed in my own thoughts, and exchanging Happy Holidays whenever I chanced to make eye contact with a familiar face. After a while, I checked the time and it was past 11. When I looked at my phone to see whether William had texted, Joe reappeared.

"There she is."

"Yes, but I was about to leave," I said, and looked at my shoes.

"What's wrong?" he asked.

"Oh, my feet hurt. It'd be nice to just take my shoes off." Right, it would. But then I would step out of my role. Should I?

"Why suffer?"

Before I said anything, he knelt and slipped them off my feet. I felt warm, but I froze, and then my body spoke.

I'm Clara. Nice to meet you, I heard it say.

"You look nice," he said, perhaps trying to make me feel comfortable with myself. And he succeeded.

Then his phone rang, and he signaled that he had to answer. He turned away and disappeared again into the party.

When my colleagues toasted Christmas at midnight, I looked for him but he was nowhere to be found. I stayed a little longer, then called a taxi, and returned home.

Before falling asleep I revisited the night, a series of images dancing in my head in no precise order. The chatter, the noise, my colleagues, the sushi, the wine, Joe, myself bare foot. My head was spinning. I must have had a glass too many. I thought about William, and fell asleep.

3

The alarm rang at 7.30 a.m., abrupt and loud.

I sat on the bed for a few minutes trying to remember what happened at the party. But then I gave up. I had so much work to do. That morning I would meet a new client.

I stayed in the shower longer than usual, trying to think about that meeting and something clever to say, but my mind was empty.

As I closed the door to my apartment, I faced a bright sun, so strong I could barely find the keyhole to lock the door. The air was warm, as it would have been on a September morning in Connecticut. And I could hear birds singing.

I decided to walk to the office to clear my head.

My neighborhood seemed different every time I walked through it. Stores opened and closed. Cafés that seemed so nice and welcoming disappeared overnight, replaced by others and others. But there was one that had been there since I moved in, a café I discovered on my first day in L.A.

As I walked through the door, the barista began

preparing my drink. She did not know my name, but she knew what I would order. A mocha coffee with whipped cream. Small. Hot. Always the same.

That morning I was the only customer, aside from two girls sitting on a sofa, chatting and laughing. I passed the time by skimming the large blackboard behind the counter and its long list of hot and iced teas, hot and iced coffees, and all possible sorts of smoothies. That also had not changed at all. I felt sleepy.

On one side of the room, there were two chairs, neither of which really matched the other or anything else in the café. And there was a relatively long and low-slung coffee table in front of them, pocked with scratches and stains. The sofa where the two girls were sitting was not antique but could have been described as old, very old. The barista was singing a Christmas carol and smiled at me when she handed me the drink.

"I hope you're not going to work today, sweetie."

I nodded that I was.

"Sorry about that. Have a nice day."

That wish caught me by surprise. It always did. Why were people in California so friendly? Someone had told me once that "warm weather keeps a person's heart warm." I would have told the person she was right, if I only remembered who that was.

The city was waking up slowly. It was almost 8.30, but there were few people on the street. So weird for a Monday morning, I thought. There was almost no traffic, the stores were not open yet, and aside from the birds, there was just a soft silence.

I saw so many places I wanted to visit, new and old ones. Soon, I thought. I'd come back soon.

And then I passed a pub and thought I saw the picture

of a face that looked familiar. After a few steps, I decided to go back and look again. The flyer posted on the door featured a jazz group and there was Joe, right in the middle of the group, holding an upright bass. The group would play that night at 9. I stepped back and looked at the sign. It said "Chris's Jazz Place." So he really was a musician.

I got to the office but the entrance was shut. The door was usually unlocked by 8 a.m., and it was well past that. I thought it might have been for the holidays, but that seemed strange. I went to the café on the ground floor and it was closed too. A note on the door read, "Closed on December 25th. Merry Christmas." Right, it was Christmas day. Monday, December 25th. The meeting was the next day. How could I have gotten that wrong? I felt stupid and sad. Maybe it was the wine.

So there I was, dressed for work, sleepy and tired. What a waste. I looked around.

I sat on a bench in front of the law firm building and let the exhaustion overtake me. I could feel the warmth of the sun on my face and my arms, and I thought it would be easy to fall asleep right there. The sun was so tempting but that area was not so. I pulled my briefcase closer to me and thought I would just sit there for a few minutes.

As I sat enjoying the sun, I heard someone playing piano, somewhere nearby. There was a light wind that seemed to be playing with the music, sometimes winning, sometimes losing. And when the wind lost, I could hear the music better. It seemed familiar. It sounded like Éric Satie. Oh, yes, Satie....

Before law school, my life was all about music, but now I rarely talked about those years, as every time I told someone that I had studied piano, they would insist that I play for them and I didn't want to. So I had to bury that part of my life.

My pianist was still learning the piece. Now I could hear it well. *Gymnopédie.* I loved that music, and abandoned myself to it. Everything around me suddenly disappeared or it became remote and safe. The music set me on a cloud, somewhere high. The world seemed so small from there.

I trusted that music. The music overwhelmed me, controlled me, and I forgot everything, forgot who I was and why I was there. And then I remembered.

Satie's *Gymnopédie.* It was relatively easy to play but so profound.

When I was a child, I would wait for each school day to end so that I could run back home, close the door to my room, and play for hours. There I was, with Satie, Debussy, Ravel, my piano, and my world to which no one else had access. And then I learned Chopin, Mussorgsky, Liszt. I loved their music, but I would always return to Satie, to close my eyes and breathe. My heart was beating Satie.

The conservatory I went to was in an old building with many floors and practice rooms, with old upright pianos, sometimes grand pianos. My favorite room, the one I always reserved, was a small one with a Kawai, a brownish upright piano built in the 70s. I loved that piano for its sound, delicate and crisp, not loud, but not shy either. And the room had a wide window that overlooked the town. I would spend my days there, sometimes forgetting to eat, and practicing for hours before meeting my teacher to review my work, her ideas and mine.

When I think of those years, I can still hear Satie, their silent soundtrack. Everything moved incredibly slowly and most of what happened, happened inside of me. The world outside might in fact be moving fast, but I did not care and wasn't there anyhow.

William was my best friend, and I sometimes shared my music with him. He was the leader of our group of high school friends and, in fact, the leader in any context or situation. We grew up together. Attended the same schools, did homework together, played together, laughed and cried. We were inseparable, and I was happy and proud of him as he was of me. He would tell people that I was a great pianist, but then with the same confidence he'd say I should be a prosecutor. And he meant it. All of it. Perhaps he thought music could not do justice for my talents, and thought my determination was the best of them. He said I could do anything I wanted to, and I believed him. In fact, back then, everything seemed possible, even becoming a famous pianist, an artist, a teacher, and maybe a prosecutor. All at the same time.

In February of my last semester in college, I was invited to a piano competition. I was skeptical or perhaps just tired for the end of the school year, but my teacher was so excited and I didn't want to let her down. We filed my program a few days later. I would play Chopin, Rachmaninoff, Liszt, and De Falla.

We spent hours and hours on the Chopin *Ballade* no. 1. My hands were too small for some of the passages and so I had to learn how to play with my entire body and how to use little tricks with my fingers to help me reach extensions that I could not otherwise reach. I loved Chopin, and even repeating two and three measures for an entire day felt exciting and rewarding.

And all those breathing exercises...Sometimes I almost forgot or deliberately stopped breathing, perhaps fearing I could lose the music I was playing any moment. So my teacher taught me how to breathe to retain what I was playing in my lungs.

We also worked on the *Piano Concerto no. 3* by Rachmaninoff. I loved playing that piece with the orchestra. The sound was full, powerful, and I was part of a group. Sometimes I felt I could leave the piano and start dancing behind the instruments, unseen, as everyone was as immersed as I was in that poetry.

Playing Rachmaninoff without the orchestra, though, felt different. At times, while playing it, I had to stop to hold back my tears. That music was so intense. It would create giant waves of emotions that would drag me under and suck the air out of my chest. And then I would stop, look at my teacher, and pretend I had made a mistake or didn't remember. She would not say a word. She would hug me and mimic a giant breath for me. I repeated after her and continued. I didn't need to explain anything to her. She knew me.

Despite the many breathing exercises, the reassuring hugs, and the pauses, controlling my emotions while playing remained hard. At times my heartbeat was so loud that I could feel it in my fingers, and when that happened, my fingers would stop.

Nothing seemed to work.

I also tried to take some distance from the music, think of myself as its narrator, someone who could tell the story of that piece to the audience without letting the story possess her. It really was hard. That music was my story, my sorrow, my desires.

But one day, I don't remember exactly when or how, I found the magic "switch," one that would make me step away from myself and just tell the story. And I could make that switch work if, while on stage, I avoided looking at the audience. I would just focus on a corner of my piano, perhaps my music stand, stare at it, and never vary my gaze.

And this is what I did at the competition. When the host announced my name and my program, I barely heard him, as busy as I was trying to detach myself from my heart or, at least, keep some distance from it.

Someone waiting close to me patted me on my shoulder, somehow waking me from my trance. I jumped on the stage breathless, almost surprised to find myself there. My eyes brushed the audience and the dark room that seemed wall-less. I grabbed my skirt tight to dry the sweat from my hands, took a deep breath, bowed to the darkness, and walked to the piano.

There was always a moment of silence before I started playing. It was me and my piano, and I would ask him to be nice to me, not to betray us and our story.

That time there was silence too. I looked for the switch, I found it, and played.

I remember how proud I was of my performance that night. I managed to be the narrator of the music, not its protagonist. I played the Chopin *Ballade,* the Rachmaninoff *Concerto*, the *Mephisto Waltz* by Liszt, and the *Ritual Fire Dance* by De Falla. It was probably my best performance ever and, in fact, I won that competition.

I remember when I checked the notice board and saw my name on top of a long list of participants. I closed my eyes, and for a few seconds I felt I was touching the sky, or shaking Satie's hand. Satie was smiling. I remember the crowd pushing me toward that notice board. Before they realized I was "Clara Smith," I had already disappeared.

I went for a long walk, alone. When I returned, my piano teacher was talking with the examiners. I could see their lips moving, but I heard no sound. I shook their hands, smiled, but I wasn't there. My teacher told me the day after that my reviews had been stellar, and that one of the examiners had invited me to study with him in Vienna and perform the same program in a concert in Brussels in late July.

I graduated from college in May and spent the next two months preparing for that.

While my classmates traveled the world as a reward for having finished college, I spent my days playing and reading.

I loved Charles Baudelaire and Oscar Wilde, and read almost everything they wrote, immersed in their stories of pleasure and beauty. At times, when I read, I had the feeling I was still playing Chopin and Rachmaninoff, as those authors had so much in common. They seemed to. But it wasn't just that. It was also the way I read those books that felt like playing them.

My father had a huge collection of old books. The pages of those books were stuck together, as he explained this was the practice in the old days. You needed to separate the pages to read them.

He showed me a knife I could use to cut the pages, and showed me how to use it. But sometimes I was so lost in the reading that I forgot what he had explained, or felt that the story or I couldn't wait the completion of that ritual. And so I used my fingers to separate the pages, and my cuts were anything but neat and precise, but as I was using my heart and my fingers, they felt right. I was playing the books.

My father never complained about my opening procedure. Sometimes he would open a book, smile, and say, "Clara read this." My mother wasn't as pleased. She thought the books were something to showcase. Not their stories. Their covers, their pages were. I should have used the knife.

One day, while working on the *Ballade* and on the hand

movements I needed to perfect, I started feeling warm, excited. I slowly lost contact with the room, felt as if I were in trance, felt warmer and warmer, and then a rush of relief. I had never experienced anything like that while playing.

I thought it might have been the heat of the room, or the long hours. Or perhaps it was Baudelaire and Wilde playing tricks on me.

You don't play books, and you don't make love to your piano. But everything seemed to be losing boundaries, contours. Everything was melting into everything else. My room, my books, my fingers, the piano, myself.

Slowly I lost interest in anything that wasn't my music and my books, and I lost the ability to communicate with the outside world. In fact, at times I felt I had left that world. And at times I was scared.

It was great to lose myself in my music without feeling overwhelmed by it. I loved that feeling, melting with my notes, losing perception of time and space. It was great, but what if something like that happened on stage, during a concert? I tried to forget that episode. Most likely, it would not repeat itself.

And soon it was time to play in Brussels.

I flew there with William, who had just returned from South America. He was so enthusiastic about his trip and a girl he had met there. He showed me photos of her, of the two of them together, sometimes sharing more than I would want to hear. I remember thinking I would have loved to spend my summer with him, traveling together through South America, rather than in the little box of my piano room. But obviously I did not tell him that and, out of the blue, made up an imaginary friend, someone I had met while he was in South America, a pianist who made me "experience life more deeply."

I don't know how I came up with that ridiculous phrase and, most of all, I don't know what I was trying to accomplish with it. The net result was that William incessantly teased me about my "new friend" and my ridiculous description. And finally, despite all my efforts to keep serious, I gave up and laughed at all his jokes. Perhaps he knew that I had made up the entire story and perhaps, by then, I felt relieved that he had.

We rented a room for two in a hotel that looked cheap and at times depressing. He had warned me that a three-star hotel would not be the ideal place to stay, but I didn't believe him, thinking he was being a snob. As it turned out, he was right, and I felt responsible for that choice. But, again, I didn't say that.

The night before the concert we went out and had a wonderful time. William had been to Brussels before and so he showed me around. I still remember *La Grande-Place* and the waffles covered with melted chocolate. And I remember the red wine with which we toasted right after that, and our mutual attraction that perhaps we both discovered that night, but decided not to confront. Or he decided not to.

We slept close to each other, and I felt a deep desire to make love to him. We joked about the fact that we were sleeping together but, no, nothing happened.

"I love that we are friends," he said, and hugged me. I felt the weight of his words on my chest, and I wished to be free of him but not of his arms.

"Sure," I replied, and made fists with my hands to trap my desire and disintegrate it.

The day after, I was more distracted than I would normally be before a concert. My performance was scheduled for nine p.m., and so William suggested that we have dinner before, and he even convinced me to have a glass of wine. I felt relaxed, much more than usual, but I thought it was OK, as the concert was a prize, not a test, an exam I had to take.

I wore a simple black dress, hoping I would turn into an invisible part of the piano. And perhaps I did at some point. Or I just felt so.

"Clara Smith," the emcee said. The audience applauded, and I walked onto the stage.

The room was so big. I broke my rule and looked at the audience. The examiner who had invited me to Vienna was sitting in the front row. I smiled at him. William was a few rows behind him. And I saw so many other faces. I still remember some of them. Their eyes seemed to be waiting for me to share what I had to share. I smiled at a girl who was holding sheet music. I could read Chopin on the cover and I thought that girl could have been me, years before. I smiled.

I turned and went to the grand piano, a majestic Steinway. I looked at it. It was silent now, but I knew its sound. I had played it before. I seated myself and felt comfortable. I closed my eyes and everything disappeared. Then I opened them and looked high, the highest I could reach. I thought about what I was going to play, the first notes over and over again, and then I started. The music pierced the silence.

Chopin.

My execution of the *Ballade* was exactly as I wanted it to be, even if I almost slipped on the last notes as I was perspiring.

The audience applauded, I sensed their enthusiasm, but it was as if it reached me from far away. I grabbed the handkerchief I had placed on a side of the music stand and dried my hands.

I took a deep breath and played Rachmaninoff. Then De

Falla.

Yes, I was pleased with my performance and I thought that the wine and the time with William the night before might have helped. I felt comfortable, happy, beautiful. I looked at my hands, my fingers, thought about Baudelaire and Wilde, opened their stories, and started the *Mephisto Waltz*.

My mind went back to William and the night before. I don't need to be here, I thought. I can execute this piece with closed eyes, and it will be perfect.

And so I closed my eyes, and felt my heartbeat. Come on, let it go, Clara. Let it go, it shouted. And I wanted to hear, I was tired of being a story-teller for that music. That music was mine.

I watched Baudelaire and Wilde's stories melt into the waltz, my soul entered, and I lost control of all.

I wrapped myself in the warmth of the feelings that were exploding in my chest. I was still playing, but I was no longer there. And I started imagining William and I making love.

Again that warmth. But I did not wake up. I kept moving, I kept playing, and I felt. I did.

The microphone on the music stand caught my heavy breath and my gasp as I woke up from my trance.

I glanced at the examiner in the front row, then at William, again at the examiner. I played a few notes, stopped for a few seconds, but then I continued. And I think I cried, those invisible, loud tears that continue to stain your face for longer than you sometime even know.

I continued playing until I completed the waltz. Then I stood up, bowed, and left the stage without looking at the audience again.

The audience applauded, but I felt I had failed. The

emcee called me back to the stage and I did go back, my face red, my body still shaking. I bowed again and left the stage quickly. The audience continued to applaud, calling me back to stage, but I left by the back door and did not return.

William found me in the alley behind the theatre. We walked in silence until we came to a park. We sat on a bench, a few feet apart. He wanted to talk about what had just happened. I did not.

"I think I might know what happened on the stage," he said, "but I might be wrong."

"I think you might be right."

"Did you...come?"

I could have thought of a million nicer ways to say that. But that was William. Straightforward, brutal, often treating me as his male buddy.

"Yes, I did."

He laughed. I cried.

"He put his arm around my shoulder, and tucked my head against his chest.

"Clara, don't worry. Shit happens. And you're an artist."

An artist....

The last day in Brussels was awful. William met an Erasmus student at a bar and he did not come back to the hotel until the day after. The papers that morning talked about the extraordinary talent of a young pianist. The big, black-and-white photo of me on stage at the end of the concert there to remind me of something I wanted to forget.

My career was ready to take off, but we flew back home that day, and I stopped playing.

I did not tell my parents what had happened in Brussels. I said I had made a couple of mistakes on Liszt and stopped playing for a few seconds. My father found it hard to believe, but said I was tired and needed a break.

I did take a break, a long one. In fact, I was still on that break.

I spent the next two years traveling nowhere special and then studying for the law school admissions test. The letter of admission came as a goodbye note to the artist.

And there I was. A lawyer. Alone on a bench, in front of the office. On Christmas Day.

"Clara, is that you?" The voice took me by surprise. I looked up.

"Joe? What are you doing here?"

"This is where I rehearse." He gestured to a small, brick building on the corner. "What are *you* doing here?"

"I work here. Well, not today. I actually forgot that today was Christmas. Is that bad?"

"Not so bad." He laughed. "Merry Christmas, by the way."

"Merry Christmas," I replied. "Your band rehearses here?"

"Yeah, in the music school over there. One of us teaches there, so from time to time they let us use a room."

"But you're playing tonight? I saw a flyer at...?"

"Yeah. The Jazz Place. Down the street. Adam said he might come." As he finished that sentence, he looked over his shoulder as if he was expecting something or someone. Then he turned back to me and added,

"Why don't you come?"

"I...maybe..."

"I saw you moving your fingers as if you were rehearsing a piano piece." He imitated my movements with his hands. "Do you play?"

"No, I don't. I did. I studied piano. But that was a different life." I couldn't believe I just said that.

"You're a pianist."

"Oh no, I'm not."

"Well, you play, right?"

"No. Not at the moment. I have a piano in my apartment, but I haven't actually played for quite some time."

"I'd love to hear you play."

My Blackberry vibrated, and I thought I should slip out of that topic. I told Joe I had to go, and wished him good luck for the concert.

"I hope I'll see you tonight," he said as I walked away. I waved to him and looked for a quiet place to check my emails. There were a few messages by a colleague from the New York office. I ignored them. And there was a group message from Adam addressed to our "team," inviting us to Joe's concert that night.

I turned off the Blackberry and hesitated a bit. I wanted to hear more Satie, so I returned to the bench hoping I could be alone with the music again, but Joe was still there. He was holding a girl's hand. She seemed to be crying or was perhaps just very sad. I slid behind a parked car, hoping to remain unseen. She was withdrawing from him as he tried to hold her. And then they hugged without commitment, she turned away, and walked to her car.

He saw me.

He turned though, and entered the door to the music school.

I stayed there for a while, revisiting in my head what I had just witnessed. The piano was no longer playing and that corner of square that had exuded music and memories only a few minutes before, now seemed empty and uninviting. I grabbed my briefcase and sleepwalked home.

The city was sleeping as well, but now that made sense. It was Christmas, an unusual one, one that I would have remembered. Although at the time, I didn't know.

4

Once home, I took off my clothes, took another shower, and then lay on the bed staring at the ceiling with my skin still wet, wrapped in a towel. I left the window of my bedroom open, the birds were still singing. I thought I heard seagulls and fell asleep. When I awoke from my nap, I had tears in my eyes, but I didn't remember dreaming. I just felt tired and disoriented. I poured a glass of wine, looked for a Satie CD I had bought when I was in law school, and let it play for a while.

I opened the window wider and looked inside of me. I tried to imagine how Satie felt when he composed that beauty. How it felt to be living his times, in Montrermatre, in Paris. The Moulin Rouge, the ballets, the theatre, the actors preparing to perform, the clubs and the bars, the dreams and the solitude, the freedom and frustration. And then I surveyed my apartment. I saw the books I brought from the office on contract formation, and felt sad. Where was the life of an artist I had dreamt of? Did Joe live that life?

I was jealous. Jealous of Joe's life. Jealous of the intensity of whatever he had with that woman I had seen that day. I wanted something like that. I needed it.

I sipped the wine and the tension softened, but the emptiness and dissatisfaction amplified.

I couldn't say if I had ever felt satisfied, complete. But if I ever did, it was only for brief periods of time, as I was constantly looking for something, something else, something different. I never understood what that was though.

The times I felt most complete were when I played. Satie, Debussy, Liszt, Rachmaninoff, Chopin. But after Brussels and my last concert, I had stopped. Still, every time I heard that music, I remembered the joy I felt. I could almost touch it. And then I saw my present void, and knew it didn't belong to me. Yet it had become my routine, my life, masked as responsibilities, maturity, what it ought to be. Truth is, there was just void and boredom. Day after day after day.

I hadn't practiced in too many years, and now playing didn't seem as natural as it did when I was younger. I looked at the upright piano in my living room. I touched it as if I wanted to caress an old friend, reassure it or myself that I would play again soon. I looked for my Satie music sheets, skimmed them, but then put them back.

I flipped through my emails and re-read the one from Adam. The Jazz Place was walking distance from my apartment. I looked at my piano and decided to go.

As I was getting ready to leave, my phone buzzed. I checked and there was a text from William.

I know I'm late. I was thinking about what to write for Christmas. It took me the whole day and I still don't know. How are you?

I stared at that text for a while. It made me happy and sad. I didn't want to rush an answer, so I placed the phone on the table, put a red lipstick on, attempted a smile, and left for the concert.

The streets were crowded with people, sounds, the aroma of hot dogs, freshly baked pastries, marijuana, alcohol. I was confused, inebriated with my own confusion, then mainly confused again, and I must have looked so when I saw Adam. He was standing in front of the Jazz Place, talking to a partner from the law firm, someone I knew of, but hadn't met. Adam whispered something to him and then came closer to say hi.

"Here she is. You won another file, my Dear."

Oh, good, I thought. More work. That's what I needed. But before I said anything, he continued.

"We need an associate to go to Italy for six months. There's a company in Siena one of our clients wants to buy. He's asked us to do a due diligence and we need someone reliable to supervise the work. I thought of you. What do you think?"

Did I hear that right? Italy? For six months?

He stared at me, his smile bigger than his face.

"So what do you think?"

"When would I go?" I asked, still unsure that I had heard it right.

"Soon. We'll work out the details over the next couple of days. We've talked with the client and briefed him on your background. He's on board, very excited about having you run the project."

I nodded with what must have been a blank expression on my face, and that seemed to make him uncomfortable.

"It'll be great," he pressed, his last unsuccessful attempt to get an enthusiastic response from me. Then he checked his watch and nudged me to the door.

"We'll chat tomorrow." He finally dropped the topic.

I didn't know what to think. I felt that something or someone other than me was directing my life again, and I had no control over it. No, I wasn't happy.

As I was immersed in my thoughts, I entered the Jazz Place and saw Joe.

He was standing on the stage together with three other guys. The body of his bass lay on the floor, the neck leaning on a wooden chair, almost a relic from an elementary school, one from a distant past. On the opposite side of the stage was a grand piano. The drum kit was aligned between the bass and the piano. And slightly to the left of the drums, a trumpet sat propped on another chair. That must be it, I thought. A quartet.

Joe was talking to a guy near the right edge of the stage. They seemed to be working on a rhythm. The guy tapped out a pattern on his leg, nodding and moving his hands so as to follow Joe's lead. They laughed and Joe whispered something. As he was leaning toward his friend, he saw me and stopped. He then smiled, raised his right hand, and signaled that he would join us soon.

There were four of us. Adam, the other partner, Lilly, who had just joined the firm, and me. We sat at a table near the stage, and ordered some drinks. Soon after, Joe came over.

"You got the best table," he said, and shook hands with each of us.

"Are you excited, man?" Adam asked.

"Always excited when I play. It's a cool set and a super band. The horn player has amazing chops. He's just back from promoting his new CD in Europe."

"What about you?" Adam asked.

"I'm just the glue that holds it together. They are the stars."

"O.K.," he then said, "sit back and enjoy the show. I'll catch you all later." He looked at me and left.

As I watched him disappear behind the stage, I looked around. The club was simple but somehow loosely sophisticated, charming, and it had now filled to capacity. The crowd was mostly in their thirties or forties. Men, women, couples, groups of friends, elegant and casual faces.

The band hadn't taken the stage, but the background music was so loud I could barely hear the table chat. Someone would say something and everyone else would smile or nod. Lilly was trying hard to get the attention of the two partners. When her eyes crossed mine, they quickly moved away. She saw what I thought.

I sipped my drink and wandered off into my own world. Then I saw Joe coming onto the stage and walking to his bass. He lifted it and cradled it in his arms. There was some silence. Then the drummer beat a five count, and it was Brubeck. *Take Five*.

The music pulled me in, I felt a surge of happiness, and felt like I wanted to dance. Meanwhile, everything around me had disappeared. The audience, the waiters, my thoughts. I closed my eyes and let myself go.

I looked at the red velvet wine in my glass and took another sip. I felt warm and thought I missed being in love. Love should taste like that wine, I thought. And it should make me feel light, happy. Did I ever feel that way? Perhaps. When I played and when William and I talked things through. I missed that.

I drifted more deeply into myself and started dancing in the club. Nobody could see me though. I was holding my dress, barefoot, bending and pirouetting on the tables, tasting people's wines, looking straight into their eyes. Yes, they could not see me.

And then that bass line. I turned and saw Joe. He was immersed in his music, the bass part of his body, its main part. He was playing with the riff and I loved it.

The instruments were talking with each other. I knew their code, their improvisation, what they were doing. I could anticipate their changes.

The trumpet took the solo.

They played a few more classics and then a set of originals, one that I particularly liked, with subtle metric changes moving smoothly from a major to a minor key. Then Joe counted four, and it was "Somewhere Over the Rainbow." Their finale. Pure magic.

I found myself staring at Joe, lost in his performance, suspended but floating. On the last note, he raised his eyes and caught mine. His gaze too deep to bear. I looked away.

When the applause faded and Joe thanked the audience, I excused myself to go outside and breathe. As I stepped past the door, I saw the same woman I had seen earlier that morning with Joe. She was wrapped in a severe black coat that was too big for her. She looked pale and fragile. As she was entering a taxi that had just pulled to the curb, Joe came out and called to her.

"Sarah, wait!"

She heard him but did nothing to stop the cab as it left. Joe stared as it drove off, and then turned and saw me. He looked down and returned to the club.

When I returned to the table, Adam and the others were celebrating a recent puff piece about the law firm's ranking. I tapped Adam on the shoulder and told him I had to go. He asked me if I needed a ride. I thanked him but explained that I lived just around the corner.

I grabbed my purse, my jacket, and headed to the door.

5

When I got home, I opened the windows to my living room, took off my shoes, and crashed on the sofa. I had not checked my phone in hours. There were no new texts, no missed calls, no new emails, except one from jgray@aol.com. Who was that?

Hi Clara,

I think you saw me with Sarah earlier today and again after the show. I need to talk to someone and I think I need a woman's point of view. No problem if you don't feel up to it though. I'd totally understand. If you do, I'll be at the club until late tonight.

Anyhow, I'm happy you came.

Take care,

Joe.

I was surprised by that email, and wondered why he needed a woman's point of view, and why this woman.

I went to the bathroom to brush my teeth and thought about it. My face in the mirror looked tired and tense. Somehow mad at someone for something, or just mad at myself.

What if I went back to the club?

As I stared in the mirror, I tried to compromise and please my face, ease its tension, make peace with it.

What if I went there now? After all, the club was close by.

But why would I do that? What was the rush? I could call him tomorrow. There was a phone number in the email. Yes, I should call tomorrow.

I didn't convince my face and I left it in the mirror. I turned, and headed to my bedroom.

As I was undressing, I looked at the watch on my night-stand. It was only 11:30.

My pajamas on the bed gave me a sense of the time that was slipping through my fingers. I'd had them for many years, and like them, not much had changed. I had slipped into routines that had made my life the most remote thing from Satie, from those times in Paris I had always dreamt of living.

I enjoyed being at the club. Why did I leave in such a hurry? I should have stayed, listened to more music, met people, talked with Joe and his friends, something. Instead, I was about to go to bed at 11:30, alone, on Christmas.

I didn't feel like sleeping.

I put on my law school t-shirt, grabbed my Blackberry, and started playing with it. And then, I don't know why or how, I dialed Joe's number. He didn't answer and I thought that was a sign that I was doing something stupid.

I turned off the light and pushed my head under the pillow to shut down my brain, but the phone rang.

"I got a call from this number. Did you call?"

I remained silent.

"Hello...?" he repeated.

"I was...."

"Clara?"

"Yes."

"You called?"

I didn't know what to say. I stayed silent, but the silence got loud.

"Clara?"

"Yes. Sorry. I . . . we could talk tomorrow."

"How about now? Where are you?"

"At home."

"Where is that?"

"Near 5th and Flower."

"That's just two blocks from here."

"Three."

"I could come get you."

"I'm in bed."

He remained silent this time, and I realized I missed hearing his voice.

"Can we talk over the phone?" I asked.

He took a deep breath.

"Sure," he said, "it's about Sarah, the girl you saw tonight and maybe this morning. She's, was my girlfriend. We've been together five years, but lately it's been tough. Actually, it's been bad for a quite a while. I've tried to fix it, but nothing works."

"And how do I fit into this?"

"Not sure. I thought I might talk to you for some reason."

I didn't know what to say. We were basically strangers.

He said something else, but I interrupted him.

"Wait," the word escaped me before I could even try to control it. "I'll come to the club. I'm awake, and I don't think this would work over the phone."

What was I doing? It was midnight, and I was on the phone with someone I had met only the evening before, talking about his girlfriend. And now I was going out to meet with him? To make it *work*?

"Great. Call when you're close."

I dressed quickly and arrived at the club in no time. I didn't call Joe again but there was no need, as when I got there, he was outside, waiting for me.

He said hi, thanked me for coming, and studied me for a beat.

"There's a quiet bar around the corner," he said.

I looked at him and lost myself.

"I know this must seem strange," he added.

Yes, it was strange.

We started walking to the bar. He seemed anxious to get there, and quickly brushed past a number of people on the street he appeared to know, as if the time we had together could expire any moment and we shouldn't waste it.

I thought of William, as this was something he would do. Call me late at night, suggest a walk and a chat, and make us the only thing that mattered. I loved when he did that. I loved the late-night chats and us becoming the only thing that mattered.

While Joe was walking slightly ahead of me, I got stuck in a clutter of people. He came back, grabbed my hand, and kept walking with my hand in his. What was happening? Everything seemed to be moving so fast. Had he decided my role in his life without even consulting me? Perhaps my eyes were asking him those questions, but he was still in front of me looking straight ahead, so he didn't see them.

When we arrived in front of the bar, I freed my hand from his, and tried to catch my mind.

"This is the place," he said.

I nodded that it was fine, and we entered.

"Two?" a woman asked, and then asked for my ID. I

wasn't surprised. Sometimes, when I wore jeans and t-shirt, I could look much younger than I was.

Joe said we were two, and I showed her my ID. She gave us a table in a quiet area of the bar, we ordered our beer, and she left.

"So...Sarah," he said.

"Yes."

Our eyes locked, and I was ready to listen.

"We met five years ago. She was a music journalist. Came to one of our gigs and wanted to interview me. She was shy, could barely ask questions. It was hard to believe she was a journalist. Somehow we clicked though, started dating a few months later, and then moved in together. She didn't like nightclubs, but this was mainly where I played. So I spent less time with her, and more time with my band. Lots of late nights and less and less in common. She felt abandoned and became more demanding. She wanted to be with me more, I wanted her less."

The waiter came with the beers. He stopped to take a sip of his, and looked into my eyes. Whatever he found in there, he decided to continue.

"Five or six months ago, I told her I was unhappy with our relationship, didn't think it was working. She didn't say a word, turned, and walked out of the room. The next day, she didn't get out of bed, and then the next and the next. She stopped eating, neglected herself, and treated me as if I didn't exist. I slept on the couch, if I slept at all. This lasted several weeks. I felt guilty and hated to see her suffer, so I told her that I loved her and promised that we'd be together forever. In fact, I didn't love her, don't love her, or at least I'm no longer in love with her. But I had to stop the hemorrhaging and this is how I did it. She perked up and went back to her daily routine. But for me everything became worse. Her cheerfulness constantly reminding me of my lie. Stupid, right?" he asked, but looked away, not really waiting for an answer.

Then he became uncomfortable, his voice dropped a tone, and sounded more strained.

"Not too long ago, we auditioned Mara. She was a natural jazz singer. We invited her to sing with us. One night, while rehearsing, she got drunk, I was drunk too, and after everyone left, we stayed, got drunker, and made love in the rehearsal room. I was in love with her voice, her music. Not with her though. And she didn't love me either. But I needed that passion, and realized what I was missing with Sarah. I'm not proud of this, but it happened. Sarah walked in on us. That was a month ago. I felt so guilty, and still do. And sometimes I miss her. But it might be shame or pity. I'm not sure what to do or what she even wants me to do. She confronts me, and then runs. Like today."

Solitude, depth, mistakes, love, and then more mistakes. Satie was playing again in my head. But this time Joe was playing it for me.

"Do you want to leave Sarah?" I asked.

"Maybe. I don't know. I have feelings for her, but I don't love her, I mean, not in the way I should or the way she would want me to. I'm not attracted to her."

He looked down, then up into my eyes.

"I trust you," he said.

"I'm still not getting it. I'm sorry. Why me?"

"I don't know. I can't explain it."

His eyes seemed sincere.

I spun my glass with my fingers and looked more deeply into the empty room searching for the answer that he had not given me, but had no luck. Then I turned to him.

"I'd probably step back," I said. "I'm going to Italy. I don't know when, but it should be soon. I could be gone for several months. If that happens, you could stay at my place. I don't want to leave it vacant. And this would help you take some distance from all of this. Understand it better. I wouldn't act until I know what I want."

So I was leaving my apartment to him. I trusted him too, but I also couldn't explain why.

"Italy? When are you leaving?"

"I'll have a better idea tomorrow."

"How do you feel about it?"

"I'm not sure. This project came as a bit of a surprise."

It must have been the beer and the fact that I was tired, but I felt I could lose my filters with him any moment, and didn't want to.

"I'd better go," I said. "Tomorrow I need to be at the office early. I'm sure you'll be fine."

He smiled and looked thankful. Then called for the check, left a few bills on the table, and waved to the waitress.

We left and walked in silence, close to one another, but perhaps distant from each other's world. At least it felt so.

But then, when we arrived in front of my place, I suddenly felt close to him again. We looked at each other and hugged. That felt real, and it felt good, too good to resist.

That night, I couldn't sleep. Not even for a minute. I felt every beat of my heart, and every beat was too loud.

6

When the alarm rang the next day, I was watching the color of the sky slowly turn from dark blue to softer, paler tones. I was awake, my eyes were open, but I felt detached from my bed, my room, my work, the plans for the week, and Italy. It was as if I was sleepwalking.

I went to the kitchen and made coffee. The aroma filled the almost empty room. Aside from a small sofa and a table, I had no furniture. Just a clutter of boxes, books, random piles of sheet music, and CDs. All on the floor. And there was my piano, a silent witness to my temporary lack of commitment. To myself.

I opened the windows and let the fresh air take over. I had lived that same scene every day since moving to L.A., but that morning something felt different, as if that air was penetrating me, almost hurting me.

I held my cup of coffee tight in both hands, and immersed my nose in it to feel the aroma more deeply. I closed my eyes and saw Joe and our hug in front of that same window.

How had we become so close so quickly?

As I was looking for answers, I pressed my hands more firmly against the cup, and it fell and spilled coffee all over the floor, on my feet, and my feelings.

I cleaned the floor, walked to the bathroom, filled the tub with hot water and soap, and immersed myself in their warmth. I then got dressed and took a cab to the office.

When I arrived, Adam and Elizabeth, the managing partner, were waiting for me in a conference room. Adam put a file on the table, looked at it, then straight at me.

"Clara, as I said last night, we need you to go to Italy and lead a due diligence team to assess whether Simi SPA is worth buying." He slid the file toward me. "It's a challenging project, but given what we've seen of your work and your drive, we think you'd be perfect for it."

Adam looked at Elizabeth for approval. She nodded and added,

"Yes, you're perfect for this. It's a lot like the work you did for me on the Ledbetter project. And this time you won't be by yourself. We'll give you a team of Italian lawyers from one of our best friends in Milan."

"Best friends" were the law firms in partnership with us. Ironically, we could barely remember their names, and most of the times, had not ever met any of their associates.

I opened the file. The work was for Pierce Downing, one of the firm's major clients. I looked up.

"O.K. I can do this," I said, as I knew I had no option. "When should I leave?"

"We'd like you to leave soon, by early February at the latest, but the sooner the better," Adam said.

I nodded, then my Blackberry vibrated to remind me of a conference call. We wrapped up our discussion and I took the file to my office.

As I looked through my emails to find the phone number and code I needed to dial to access the call, I noticed a text from Joe. He said he had news and asked if you could talk. I said it was O.K., and we agreed to meet that night at 9.30 at the Jazz Place.

I accessed the conference call and announced my presence. I set my phone to speaker and looked for a notebook to take notes, but the call continued essentially without me. Although I did my best to focus, it was just too hard. I vaguely gathered that a German company had to recall some of its cars from the market. They were talking about liability, damages, when to do what.

"Clara, what do you think?"

Oh, no. What was I going to say now?

"I think this is a nuanced and complex situation. I need to give it some thought. I'll read the file and write a memo for the group."

I never wrote that memo. And the recall file is still on my kitchen table, close to the Prada shoe.

I finished the call, checked my emails, and saw one from Adam. He said they had a problem and needed me to leave for Italy by Friday. Perhaps I could stay only for a few weeks, then return to L.A. to clean up any loose ends at work, then head back for the long haul. Without even thinking about it, I said I could do that, but asked if I could take the rest of the day off. Adam said he was happy to hear that, and gave me the rest of the week. He said Carla, my assistant, would arrange flights and accommodations, and that I would have an apartment in Siena until at least August. I left the office right away.

I walked home listening to my iPod and brushing with my eyes places I had planned to visit but that now would have to wait. Life rarely goes according to plans. I was going to Italy.

When I arrived at my apartment, I felt relieved. Relieved to be away from work, and relieved for not having to unpack my boxes, place my books on the shelves, clear my question marks, and settle. I could put everything on hold, once again.

As I was lying on the sofa, trying to decide what to do next, my phone rang. It was Joe.

"Is it a good time to talk?"

"Yes, I'm home."

"Not working?"

"No. My boss gave me the week off since I'll be leaving for Italy this Friday."

"I didn't know you'd be leaving so soon."

"Me neither. But something happened and they need me there immediately."

"Are you O.K. with that?"

"It's fine."

There was some silence.

"Listen," he then said, "you don't have to let me use your apartment. That's generous, and I truly appreciate it, but it's way too much."

"No, it would actually help if you stayed here. But I don't think I can come to the club tonight. Too much to do between now and Friday."

"Makes sense. Should I come see the apartment before you leave? Tonight maybe?"

That caught me by surprise but I thought I should meet with him. He said he could come sometimes after eight p.m. and we agreed to meet then.

I lay on the sofa, my chest pulled by excitement and fear,

my heart in between. Too light to feel the ground, but too heavy to fly. I fell asleep and took a long nap.

When I woke up, I checked my emails and there was one from Carla. Attached, a one-way flight ticket to Firenze, and a note that I might want to take a car from there to Siena.

I took a shower, dressed, and called my parents. My father picked up the phone, and I told him about Siena. He sounded surprised and sad, hard to say whether he was more the one or the other.

"We were hoping to see you for New Years. It didn't seem Christmas without you," he said. "How long will you be gone?"

I said I didn't know. Maybe six months.

We changed the subject, chatted for a few minutes, and then said our good-byes. As I hung up, I had to shake off the guilt I felt. I hadn't seen my parents in a long time, as every time I thought of going, there was more work to do, a new file, a new client, another meeting, and my visit to them would be postponed. I knew my mother didn't miss me that much or perhaps just didn't show it. My father, though, did.

I took a deep breath and looked around my apartment, a home that never felt so. It was time to start packing again, and I wasn't even sure how long I'd be gone.

I looked for my biggest suitcase, the one I'd used to move in from Connecticut, and found it stuffed into a corner of my closet. It was old and bruised, but large and dependable. I dragged it out to the living room and opened it. It was meant for the big moves. Was this a big move?

When I opened my suitcase, I found an old photo of me and William. He had given that to me before leaving for med school. On the back he'd written, "I will miss my little Jiminy Cricket."

This is what he called me. But in truth, I wasn't wise. I

just knew him, cared about him, and loved listening to him and helping him. And he did the same for me when I let him. So, in a way, he was my "Jiminy Cricket" too. Although I never told him that, perhaps too proud to admit it, or simply afraid I could lose him if he discovered that I needed his guidance at least as much as he needed mine. Apparently, though, my endeavors had not been successful, since we had lost each other. And I had lost a big part of myself with it. I wondered if he felt the same.

I looked at the photo again. We looked so happy, standing in front of our high school building, hugging and laughing, seated on his old motorcycle, too small to accommodate two people, and yet just perfect for us.

I could not erase him from my memories. I didn't want to. So I returned the photo to the suitcase and started packing.

I gathered business suits and casual clothes. The suitcase was only half-full, but I thought I had all I needed. More, actually.

I put on some music, and started cleaning the apartment. I cleaned, checked emails, cleaned more. From time to time I'd remember another shirt or pants, pull them out, and place them in my suitcase. By the time I was done cleaning, not much was left in the closet and drawers. I seemed to be moving out.

I thought about working on the car-recall file I had taken home with me, but then resolved to fly back east to visit my parents before leaving for Italy. I went on the internet and found a round trip from L.A. to New Haven, leaving the next morning and returning the following day, Thursday, late afternoon. I bought the ticket, and informed my father.

When it was half past eight, the doorbell rang.

I ran to the door and saw Joe standing behind the glass. His face cast downward, his hands in his pockets. He raised his eyes to look at me. He was overwhelmingly handsome.

"Hey," he said. His voice low and deep as I remembered.

"Please come in."

"So you're leaving Friday, huh?"

"Actually, I'm leaving tomorrow for a quick trip home before I go to Italy."

"Where's home?"

"New Haven."

"You'll fly to Italy from there?"

"That would have been the smartest thing to do, but reservations to Italy were set before I decided to visit my parents. So I'm flying to New Haven tomorrow, early in the morning, I'll be back Thursday evening, and then off to Italy the next morning"

"You'll be exhausted."

"I'll be sitting the whole time, reading and watching movies. I've done worse."

He looked around, and gazed at the boxes on the floor.

"Are you moving out?"

I smiled.

"No. I actually brought these from Connecticut when I moved in. I haven't had the time or motivation to unpack, and now it turns out I'm leaving again. Ironic, isn't it?"

"Not ironic. Maybe fun."

No, I didn't think so.

He went to the living room window and stood exactly where I had stood earlier that morning. He stared out. Did he see our hug too? When he turned to look at me I feared he might have, so I turned away.

"Let me show you around," I said, moving to the kitchen.

"I'm sure there isn't much I need to explain here. Oven,

fridge, freezer." I bent over and showed him some drawers in the left corner. "If you need pans they're all here. The glasses are up there, cups...."

He took my arm and said,

"Thanks for doing this."

I turned to him and now we were too close. A strong desire to kiss him took over. I was scared and moved away to hide it.

"You said you wanted to tell me something," I tried.

"Yes, I did. Sarah and I talked today. I told her I was going to take a break from our relationship and said I would stay at a friend's place for a while. She seemed somehow prepared for this."

I raised my heels to reach the toaster on a shelf. He put his arm around my waist and pulled me against him. I could feel his breath on my neck and I froze.

"I'll stop if you want me to." He paused and then asked, "Do you want me to?"

No, I didn't.

I stopped breathing. My heart accelerated. He turned me toward him and kissed me. I lost myself somewhere. We made love. And it was heaven.

7

The night became darker, soundless. My window was open and the night air drifted through the apartment. I started feeling cold and I reached for a sweater. I checked the clock on the side of the bed. It was one a.m. In three hours, I would leave for the airport.

"How do you feel?" he asked.

"Confused." I turned to face him, seeking the courage to say what I had in mind.

"Joe?"

"Yes?"

"I usually don't..."

He pulled me to him, pressed his body against mine, and kissed me. Then he looked at my eyes, deeply into them, and kissed me again.

He wanted to take me to the airport but I told him I needed some time for myself. We remained silent, holding each other for a while, and when it was two a.m., he left and I remained alone. I made coffee and sat on my bed, trying to make sense of what had just happened.

I stuffed some underwear in my backpack, two t-shirts,

my computer, looked for my heavy coat, called a taxi, and waited. At a little after four, the taxi arrived and I surrendered to its consumed, faux-leather seats.

The city seemed different. Everything did.

Homeless people were dragging themselves and their carts filled with nonsense along empty streets. They seemed artists lost in the madness of their art. Had they been loved? Were they in love now? What genius did their costumes betray?

I did not know I could make love as I made love to Joe. I did not know someone could make love to me as he did. I kept waiting for something like this to happen. I just wasn't sure it was possible. I thought it would take time to feel how I did, and yet everything happened so fast. Still, it seemed right, natural. Could someone fall in love that quickly? Was I in love? Was I mad?

At the airport, I checked in, boarded, and fell asleep before the captain said we were taking off, assuming that he did. I cannot recall. We landed in Philadelphia, and from there I took my connecting flight to New Haven. I slept on that flight too. But again, I don't even remember boarding that plane.

When I arrived in New Haven, my father was waiting for me. We hugged and he told me how happy he was to see me. I was happy too, somehow safe from my confusion.

We walked to his car and he said that my mother was home, making dinner, "a surprise." I was happy to hear that, as I needed to talk to him alone. I would have not told my mother what happened or sought her advice. We never shared anything that intimate. It was different with my father, although this topic would be unusual for us too.

"How are you?" he asked. "You must be excited about Italy."

"Should I be?"

"Why not?"

I didn't respond, and gazed into space, my eyes clouded.

"You look tired," he said.

"It's been a tough few days."

"Are they overworking you?"

When the traffic light turned red, he turned toward me, waiting for me to talk.

"It's not work. It's something else."

I glanced up at him, but neither of us spoke. Then the light turned green and he continued to drive.

My father would be fifty-seven in January, but he looked much younger. His hair had not yet turned grey and he kept in shape by exercising regularly, almost obsessively. He was an attractive man, open and comfortable with himself. But sometimes he slipped into a silent sorrow, and if I tried to enter, he would kiss my forehead, perhaps silently asking me to leave.

His life seemed to have been carefully planned, with only a few surprises and detours. There was college, travel, teaching, marriage, and me. His relationship with my mother seemed to have been planned too, and it showed no sign of passion. He was always kind to her and treated her with respect. But romance did not seem to be part of their picture. I thought that was probably normal for a couple that had been together for almost thirty years. I tried to imagine if they might have ever felt for each other what I felt for Joe, at least at the beginning of their relationship, but I couldn't. My mother had aged worse than my father, and I sometimes wondered whether he had ever been attracted to other women during their marriage, if he had an affair. But that seemed unlikely. He lived his life in his job and his family, and seemed fine with it.

When I was home, we were often together, playing tennis and basketball, talking about my dreams and disappointments. He rarely talked about himself though. He listened to me and talked to me about me. I thought that was what a father would do. But I wished he had shared with me more of himself than he actually did. One time, though, he told me how fascinated he was by the planets and how they moved, and by the black hole. He said he had been thinking about the mystery of life and had to admit to himself that there was something bigger than us, something spiritual that was moving everything, us. That exchange was beautiful, and I remember thinking I would have loved to have more of that. But he was often lost in his silences, and when we cracked them, we almost always filled them with me and my stories.

As I was thinking about my father's mystery, he took me back to my own.

"Do you want to talk about it?"

I looked at him and missed William.

"I made love to a man I barely know," I said, and cried. And I didn't cry because I felt I had done anything wrong, but perhaps because I felt I had betrayed a dream, an idea, something.

My father stopped the car, parked on the side of a street, and called my mother. He told her I had to run some errands and we would be home soon.

He placed his arm around my shoulder and, without saying a word, walked me to a café he knew I liked, one where I used to go to study. When we entered, the woman behind the counter recognized me but barely acknowledged my presence. Polite but distant. This is how I remembered her.

My father ordered two hot chocolates, "with a lot of

whipped cream on top," and when we sat I told him about Joe, how he and I met, our chats, his concert, his music, his complicated relationship with Sarah, my offer to him to stay at my apartment while I was in Italy.

"What do you like about him?" he asked.

"I love his silences. It's what he doesn't say but somehow expresses. I feel there is more in his heart that I want to explore. I feel that I know him even if I don't. And I feel that he knows me, but can't explain why. I love his music, the way he feels it. I love the way he took care of his girlfriend." I reached out for his hand.

"Can you love someone you barely know?"

"I think so," he said, and sounded more confident than his words. But he looked distracted, lost in a thought.

"If you made love to someone you thought you loved, you didn't make a mistake," he added. Yes, he sounded confident. But why? Would he tell me?

I took a big spoon of whipped cream and sank into its softness. I felt like a young girl with her father explaining the world to her, a world that perhaps he himself didn't know that well. But I trusted him, as he often knew things I didn't know, and could unfold them for me and make me believe that everything was going to be fine no matter what.

I remembered the time I fell from my first bike, and skinned my knee. He took me to a diner, bought me a banana split bigger than me, and then took me back to where I fell to show me how to avoid making the same mistake again. This time, though, I might have not made any mistake. Did I?

He tasted his chocolate and seemed again lost in his thoughts. Then he looked back at me.

"Have you thought about your birthday at all?" he asked.

I had completely forgotten. My birthday was Thursday,

in fact, the next day. I had stopped celebrating my birthdays when I was in law school. The last time I celebrated one I was with William. He had knocked on the door of my law school dorm with a cake and a flower. A daisy. He would never forget any of my birthdays, and I never forgot his. Birthdays hadn't exactly been the same since then.

"No, I wasn't planning anything," I said, and he smiled. I wondered if he knew.

We stayed at the café a little longer, talked about Italy, where I'd be staying, places I could visit in my free time, food I might want to try. He seemed to know Siena well. I asked him about it.

"Post-college travels. A different life," he said, and looked sad.

Did he miss the travels, the adventure, someone? I wanted to ask him more, but he had entered his silence again, so I changed topic, as I didn't want to leave him there, and that seemed the only way to bring him back to me. Felt so.

I asked him about himself, how school was going. He taught physics at a college in New Haven. He loved teaching and had wonderful students. Talking about them seemed to make him happy. I also asked him about my mother. He said she was doing well. She was busy remodeling the house and was spending more time with Emma, a friend of hers I had not met, an interior decorator. He described how funny the two of them looked at times, both wearing big hats with all sorts of things on top, birds, flowers, even fake glasses. We laughed and I soon forgot about my problems and felt much lighter.

When we arrived home, my mother was standing on the porch, and waved as we pulled into the driveway.

"Clara! I'm so happy you're back. You look a bit tired."

"She's travelled basically all day. Of course she looks tired, Miriam," my father said, trying to take some of her attention away from me.

"Of course," she said, and smiled. "I hope you're hungry. I made *gnocchi*!"

I love *gnocchi*. When we lived in Hartford, my mother learned how to make *gnocchi* from an Italian neighbor, Maria, my babysitter. Maria taught me many Italian words and some songs. I often spent my mornings with her when my mother was running errands. Sometimes she would make a rounded cake with a hole in the middle, a *ciambella* as she would call it. I loved it. Her husband, Alfredo, was always away. They did not have kids and she felt alone and loved to take care of me when my parents couldn't. Maria taught my mother how to make *gnocchi*, *pizza*, and *frittata di cipolle*. I loved that too. We lived in Hartford until I was ten, and then moved to New Haven when my father got transferred there. I saw Maria less and less after that, but I remember feeling so sad when my father told me she had died. The aroma of *gnocchi* in the house had brought those memories back. And I missed her.

I left my backpack on the floor of the living room and headed upstairs to my room. My bedroom was in the attic and had a small window from which I used to spy on Pete, the boy who lived across the street. I had a crush on him when I was nine or so. Pete was now married with kids, but I still teased him about my crush every time I saw him. It made him uncomfortable, and that made me smile.

My bed was against the wall, with a little nightstand to its right, an old light on top, and the last book I had read before moving out. *The Lover*, by Abraham Yehoshua. I remember reading that book in a single night and feeling deeply moved. It was exactly where I had left it. In fact, everything was.

I lay on my bed and looked around. My bedroom was my secret, safe place. I always felt nothing bad could happen to me while I was there. I would close the door, turn on my stereo, and read or play the piano for hours until my mother would call me for dinner.

My piano was across from my bed, the metronome on top, close to the Ravel and Debussy sheet music, the ones I could still play without practice. I kept them there and put Liszt, Rachmaninoff, and Chopin away. Those demanded more work and I didn't want to feel frustrated every time I returned home and discovered that I could not play them as I once could.

On my wall there were several pictures of me with high school friends. William was in almost every one. Those pictures reminded me of something beautiful I'd been, something I had been part of. My friendship with William.

Right, William. I had not yet answered his text, but I didn't feel like it. I checked my Blackberry to read that text again, and found one from Joe. It just said, "I am thinking of you," but that was enough to shake me.

My mother called from downstairs. Dinner was ready. I washed my hands and joined my parents.

I had not eaten in two days and I was starving. My mother asked me about work, but then interrupted my answers again and again with other questions or observations on completely different topics. This was her pattern. Interested, loving, but easily distracted by herself or her own thoughts. After dinner, I sat on the kitchen table right in front of the sink and watched her rinse the dishes before placing them, one by one, in the dishwasher. That was our routine when I was a child. I would watch and listen as she worked and talked, usually with her back to me. That night she told me about Emma, her new friend, and how Emma was helping her remodel the house. She asked me if I had noticed the new carpet in the living room, the new chest of drawers at the entrance, and a painting in the hall. "They are antiques," she said, emphasizing that they were important pieces of furniture and how come I had not noticed them. No, I hadn't. My mind was really somewhere else. But she didn't know that.

"Yes, I thought something was different," I said, but smiled to confess that, in fact, I had not seen any of the things she had just described. "O.K., I'll look at them carefully. But promise me you won't touch my room."

"Why? You don't trust my taste?"

"No, I trust your taste, but it feels good to come home and find my room as I left it."

"She's right, Miriam. We shouldn't touch her room. There is so much more you...we can do around the house. We really don't need to change Clara's bedroom. Don't you agree?"

"Sure," she replied. "I understand. I won't touch your room."

"Thanks, mom," I said, and kissed both of them goodnight.

When I was back in my room, I sank into my feelings for Joe. They were dancing above me and looked both real and fake, as when I tried to catch them I failed, or I didn't, but then they seemed to evaporate too quickly in my hands, as something with no texture or substance. How much did I know about him, really? Was I in love with him or with an idea of him? I did not know what he liked, how he spent his days, whether he liked talking on the phone, reading, watching old movies, new ones, comics. I had just made love to him, and I didn't know him. And what about Sarah and Mara? Where did I fit in? I was ready to give up when my Blackberry vibrated. It was him.

Can we talk?

I dialed his number and called him without thinking about what I would say.

"Hi." My voice was trembling.

"Hey." His was warm and pulled me back to the night before.

"Yes..." I felt shivers all over, but remained silent, and he continued.

"How are you?"

"Good."

There was more silence, but then he broke it.

"God, this seems strange. I've been in a haze all day, like a stupid teenager. Who are you?"

I could hear him breathing. My mind and heart were racing. Would I fall in love with him and then lose him? Would he betray me after I surrendered? Was I another Mara?

I wished I could turn down my feelings. They were so loud I could barely think or speak. And so I didn't. I needed silence, and I think he sensed that, as he didn't say much, just asked if he could see me the next day. I said he would, of course he would. I needed to see him. But I was scared.

"O.K.," he then said. "You must be exhausted. We did not sleep last night and you had a long flight. I'll let you go."

We wished good night to each other and I hung up.

I stared at the ceiling for a while, thinking about him, and running my fingers through his voice, his eyes. I could almost touch them. They had been so close to me the night before.

Then I took the *The Lover* in my hands, skimmed its

pages, and re-read some of my favorite passages. My Yehoshua times were interesting. I remembered them.

It was May, and I'd go for long walks, looking for jasmine, as one could find jasmine in New Haven.... I was a dreamer. I had just graduated from law school, and the bar preparation class would start in a week. I had one week for myself. One week only. And yet it felt longer than that before it started. Way longer. I was surprised when it was over. One week.

I met someone at the computer lab. He was working on his Ph.D. I was there to check emails. He asked me out but I wasn't even sure that he had, until we actually went out, and he said we were on a "date." He asked me if I was free that afternoon, then if I liked to read, then if I didn't mind going with him to a book festival, and then whether I was hungry and could grab a bite with him as he was. Hungry. I wasn't attracted to him, but I was looking for jasmine, I wanted to fall in love, and I thought I could give him a chance.

When we arrived at the book festival, he seemed more interested in the books on display than he was in me. We walked through the stands, and after a while, we stopped in front of one. He picked up a copy of *The Lover*, and said I should absolutely read it. I bought the book, as I was trying to fall in love. And I did. I fell in love with the book, and never saw that guy again.

I skimmed the pages of my memories, I remembered some more, but my memories faded and faded until I slowly fell asleep.

The next day, my mother woke me up with a little birthday cake and two candles, one bearing a "2" and the other an "8." My father gave me a diary with a green leather cover "for your travel memories." I thought that was sweet.

I got dressed and we left home soon after to go to our

favorite breakfast place. We stayed there for a while chatting, and then headed to the airport. I was happy to see them and see that they looked happy.

While we were waiting for my father in the car, my mother looked at me, straight into my eyes.

"You know, Clara," she said, "I never tell you this enough, but I'm very proud of you. You have developed into a wonderful woman. And you'll find love soon. Just take your time. Don't rush it. Finding true love is not as easy as it seems."

She surprised me with that. Not like her at all.

"Right, it doesn't seem easy," I said.

She smiled at me and touched my face. I smiled back and lowered my head to feel her touch more deeply.

8

The return flight to Los Angeles seemed endless. I somehow felt empty inside, and my feelings for Joe and my doubts seemed louder in my own desert.

When I got back to the apartment, I double-checked my packing, added a few things, then looked for something else to do before leaving, but I seemed to be done. So I called Joe.

I was exhausted and now, for some reason, I wasn't sure I wanted to see him. These feelings came on fast, and I was afraid that seeing him would now make it too hard for me to leave and commit to that trip. But I dialed his number and waited for him to answer. I was in turmoil. He did not answer and I started to cry, maybe because I was tired, or perhaps because now the room seemed so empty, and I felt confused and scared. But then my Blackberry rang, and I picked it up.

"Clara...?"

I was trying to dry my tears and recompose myself before saying anything, but then I answered, and my voice revealed the tears.

"Why are you crying? What's going on?"

"You didn't answer the phone...I don't know."

"I'm down the street. I was just parking my car."

"Here?"

"Yes."

I went to the door, opened it, and abandoned myself and my heart into his arms.

"I've missed you," he said.

I had missed him too, but didn't say it. I just pressed my head against his chest and remained silent.

"Are you ready to go?"

"I think so."

I looked at my apartment. It seemed emptier than when I bought it.

"Then we should go for a walk."

I nodded and we left.

We walked in silence for a while, neither of us knowing exactly what to say. I was about to leave and he would stay. It wasn't easy.

The streets were no longer celebrating the holidays, or at least it felt so. Everything seemed back to normal, real, less charming than that night we met at the jazz club.

He steered me to the door of a small café tucked into an alley, and suggested that we stop there. I must have walked past that café a hundred times, but never noticed it. We entered through a door that was so low Joe had to duck to avoid hitting his head.

The owner was an elderly Japanese man, who seemed the fading shadow of another time. As we entered, he stepped forward to welcome us, and bowed politely. He and Joe seemed to know each other and they exchanged a few words in Japanese. That was something new. What else I didn't know about him? Too bad, as now there was time to find out, to find him.

The radio was playing jazz and, from time to time, it would whisper the names of the songs it had just played.

I looked around the room. It was furnished in wood, all well-worn, aged with beauty. There were a few tables, chairs, and a small counter. Paper lanterns scattered around made a soft, orange light. And an incongruous cuckoo clock on the wall tick-tocked the hour. Everything in the room seemed to move to the beat of that clock.

And there was this strange little aquarium, an oversized wine glass, maybe three times as the size of a normal glass, filled with water, colorful sand, and a leafy, green plant. Inside, a red fish was swimming in circles, trapped in his little wine glass home. Did he know that his space was so small? Could he see the world beyond the glass?

I sat at one of the tables while Joe ordered for us. A middle-aged man sat tucked in one corner, leafing through the pages of a newspaper and sipping his tea. Almost a still life, I thought.

And I noticed ivy crawling up the walls. So I closed my eyes to see if I could feel its scent, and I did. It was light, but not entirely covered by the aroma of tea that pervaded the room. The green of the ivy was refreshing, and wrapped the café. A perfect addition to that unexpected mountain-cottage, I thought, a witness to the passing time.

"What do you think?" Joe asked, as he brought our drinks to the table.

"I like it. Very much. How did you find it?"

"I've been coming here for years. Seems part of me. I have no idea how I found it. Sometimes Yuki and I talk jazz late into the night, waiting for the sun to rise. We don't say much, as he doesn't know English, and my Japanese is too basic. But somehow we talk. And he makes me feel good. I feel safe here." He smiled, but looked sad.

"I hope you like herbal tea."

"I do. Thanks"

We sipped our tea and, for a while, remained silent, listening to the music that we both loved. Joe was probably waiting for me to talk, and I eventually did.

"Do you think he's happy in that little space?"

"Who?"

I pointed to the red fish in the wine glass. He turned to look.

"I doubt it."

He then scanned my eyes, trying to read them, but I'm sure without success, as I myself would have probably failed.

"When will you be back?" he then asked.

"I don't know."

"Isn't it a round trip?"

"Not exactly."

"You are coming back, right?" he asked.

"I don't know how long the project will take. I have an open ticket."

His mood shifted and he seemed to back away from me. He probably didn't move an inch, but I felt the space between us expand. Perhaps it wasn't the news I had delivered, as much as the way I had delivered it.

"Are you happy to be leaving?"

"I feel that I should go. I don't know if I'm happy. But I've committed to this project, so I should honor my commitment."

He placed his hand on mine, but his touch didn't warm me up.

Yuki came to ask us if we needed anything else, and when he left, I asked Joe about Sarah.

"Did you see her while I was away?"

"Sarah? Why do you ask?"

My question pierced his heart or mine.

"Actually, I did. She tracked me down at a friend's house. And we talked."

"You didn't mention that."

"No, I didn't. I thought it unimportant. You were with your family. I didn't want to burden you with my problems."

"Why did she come?"

"She felt lonely, and she wanted to cry. So I let her cry. Then we talked and she left."

He looked directly at me, but I didn't react, and he didn't say more.

We finished our drinks, each immersed in separate thoughts that felt like walls we had built to protect us from each other. I wonder if we ever crossed them.

He asked for the check, paid, and we left.

We walked back to my apartment, sometimes brushing against each other, feeling almost sorry when that happened.

The moon was full, so I didn't turn on the light when we got to my apartment.

I sat on the sofa, he came closer to me, and started undressing me. I didn't feel the excitement of our first night, but I did feel his warmth again, and for a few moments, I felt warm too. He tried to walk me to the bedroom, but I resisted. And so we made love on the sofa. It was intense, but fast. Almost frantic.

As we finished, I felt tears on my face, but the room was dark enough so I don't think he saw them.

I pulled a blanket from a corner of the sofa to cover us,

and we remained under it for a while, one close to the other.

"I feel something's wrong," Joe finally said. "What is it?"

I took a deep breath, trying to decide what to say, looking for the right words, the ones that would do the least harm, but there seemed to be none.

"I wasn't expecting this. Not now. I haven't been with anyone for a long time. And I want it, but I'm afraid. Not even sure what it is. I have to leave, and I don't really know you, or when I'll be back, and I'm unsure of myself. So what should I feel? And then there is Sarah, Mara....Who am I in all this?"

He stood up, and walked to the window.

"Yeah, I get it. It's going fast. It's taken me too by surprise. But let's not fight. You're leaving tomorrow."

"I'm not trying to fight. I'm just not sure I can trust your feelings for me."

I wished I could have taken those words back, but they filled the space between us, and echoed and echoed. And that echo started hurting me probably more than it hurt him.

"You don't...trust me?"

I wished he had asked that question differently, but I felt I should give him an honest answer, the only one I could offer at that time, and so I said,

"No, I don't."

He put on his clothes, placed the keys to my apartment on the table, and walked out the door. I let him leave without saying another word. It wasn't my pride. I just wasn't brave enough to speak.

If I close my eyes, I can still feel the pain I felt in my chest when he closed the door behind him. It hurt so much I could barely breathe. I felt alone, empty. That emptiness that feels cold and hopeless.

I closed the windows, made some chamomile tea, grabbed another blanket from my bedroom, and sat on the sofa trying to find some peace somewhere in my mind, something that would reassure me that, after all, everything was going to be fine. But I started crying, and it was hard to stop. All of a sudden, everything seemed nonsense. The suitcase on the floor, the boxes, the empty shelves.

I held my tea tight in my hands, trying to get the strength to focus, and regain balance or control.

I looked at my suitcase on the floor. It was ready. There was nothing left to do. I saw the box for the Prada shoes on the table. Only one shoe was in it. I did not know where the other one was. I was tempted to look for it, but felt too exhausted to care and, after all, nothing was perfect, and I should probably stop trying to make it appear as if it were.

I looked for something to do, something to read or listen to that would distract me and let me drift into sleep, but nothing seemed to work.

Then I found something. Right on top of a partially unpacked box, I saw a book that looked familiar. I freed myself from the blankets and went closer to check it. It was my high school journal. I didn't remember taking it with me to L.A., but apparently I had. And behind that journal, there was my law school journal. I took both of them and was about to place them in my backpack. Maybe I could read them on the plane. But then I thought that skimming them might help.

I placed the tall white cup of chamomile on the coffee table, pulled my blankets around my shoulders, and started reading.

September 5, 1992

I met William today. He is a bit chubby but looks so confident about himself. He asked me if he could sit next to me and I said that it was O.K. He seems smart, but might be someone who wants to sit next to good students to pick their brain or something. He made me laugh for the whole class though, so it's probably good that we sit together. We'll see how it goes.

November 2, 1992

William and I studied together. We did English and Math and it was fun. He told me about Susan and her boyfriend. He's ten years older. William said that he saw him once and he looked weird. He asked me if I had ever had a boyfriend and I said I did. I didn't feel like telling him the truth 'cause I want him to assume that I'm experienced and that he can talk to me about this kind of thing. David invited us to his party, and since I don't have anyone to go with, William said we could go there together as his girlfriend cannot make it. This is certainly not a date. I would never date William. But I thought it was nice of him to offer to take me there.

On that same page, there was a photo of me, William, and other classmates. We were singing something and laughing. We looked ridiculous but I loved that picture. I had completely forgotten about Elisa and Marc. I wondered what they were doing and where they were.

I skimmed more pages of the journal. My daily reports were telegraphic, and I had to pause, from time to time, and ask my memories to fill those pages with the many missing details, the unintentional and the intentional oversights.

I read about the time William and I were called on by our Math teacher and were completely unprepared, and how we tricked him into excusing us from class. The time we went to a party and stayed up late chatting and drinking the beer he somehow had managed to buy. The time we prepared our last finals and fell asleep on my bed hugging each other. The time he confessed to me that he felt something for a girl. The time I confessed to him that I had a crush on my physics teacher and he encouraged me to tell him. The time we talked about our dreams and what we wanted to do with our future. Brussels and my concert. The time William lost his grandmother. The time I lost mine. And then, finally, the description of the day William and I stopped talking to each other. I read it slowly and then I remembered.

It was Christmas. I had completed my last finals of my first semester in law school and he had completed his own finals in med school. I was waiting for him to come pick me up at home to go to a bar, get a beer, and celebrate. He came late. He seemed happy and slightly drunk. At first, I did not notice that or, at least, I did not pay close attention to him. He used to drink, but not that much, just enough to be a little over the top, especially when there was something to celebrate. And we did have something to celebrate.

My law school classmates would be with their boyfriends and spend Christmas with them. I was by myself, still single, but I had William, and I was looking forward to being with him.

When he saw me, he said I looked beautiful and I felt happy. He had told me I looked beautiful before, but this time it seemed different, real. He drove to the bar but there was no place to park, so we decided to stop at a liquor store, grab some beers, and drink them in the car while looking at the stars.

We drove to our favorite spot, one from which you could see the city. He stopped the car, handed me a beer, got one for himself, and we toasted to the successful end of our semesters and to our friendship. We talked about the problems he was having with his brother, people who were hard to deal with in school. I told him about law school, my doubts about it. We hugged and stayed there, looking at the stars, feeling happy and grateful for each other. The radio was playing Christmas songs, and it started snowing. Two beers later for him, and half one for me, he said,

"I hope we'll always be friends." And then he looked at me and kissed me. A real kiss.

I was surprised and I must have looked so when he let me go to breathe.

"I'm sorry," he said. "That was a mistake. I should have not.... I must be drunk. I'm sorry. I'll take you home."

He turned on the car and we drove in silence. It often happened that, after having a drink together at night, he would take me home and then go to a party or to a pub to meet with his pals. But when he did that, he would share his plans with me. That night, though, he didn't. At three a.m., after leaving me home, he went to a party. But I didn't know then, and I left thinking that he would go home, or somewhere, and think about what had just happened. This is what I would do, and this is what I did, as I needed to think things through. I thought he would do the same. But he didn't.

I felt like no time had passed since that night in Brussels, in that cheap hotel room. And, in fact, it wasn't just me. Both were attracted to each other, and perhaps both had been so since that night, or some time before then. I spent the night half awake, half sleeping, feeling deeply excited and confused at the same time. I knew William had a lot of girlfriends. A kiss would not normally mean much to him. I knew that. We talked about it. But I wasn't one of his girlfriends. I was his best friend.

I must have fallen asleep when the sun rose, so when I woke up, only a few hours later, I felt tired but happy, and I stayed in bed longer than usual reading a novel. Later, I received a text from Matt, a mutual friend from high school.

He was studying math at Berkeley and had just returned home for Christmas.

William and I went to this party last night. Where were you? He wandered off with some strange girl he'd just met. He texted me that he had a once in a life experience with "an expert." I wish you had been there. We would have had so much fun laughing at him.

It was snowing. And although I was in bed when I read that text, my body still warm under the blanket, I felt as if the snow had fallen all over me, freezing every part of me. I felt stupid, empty, betrayed. My best friend, someone I had grown up with, someone I thought I deeply knew and deeply trusted, had just betrayed me.

That day William texted me and looked for me almost obsessively. He called my cell, left voicemails, called me at home. I told my parents to say I wasn't in, and I hadn't seen him since that Christmas.

I entered a deep silence, deeper than anyone I had been in before, and now I felt I had never left that silence, or that it had never left me.

I turned the page of my journal and read more. That entry had a title.

Thoughts in a bottle.

I'm slowly learning to play the silence and thoughts-in-a-bottle game. I loved listening to my thoughts and my feelings flowing out of Debussy or DeFalla. I liked feeling alive. But now that I'm not playing and William's gone, I'm learning to play the silence game, and I often stare at nowhere, imagining to be somewhere else, where my thoughts dance, cry, and laugh loudly, and have fun. Here, though, now, my thoughts should stay in a bottle, for them or myself to be safe.

. . .

I can't forget them, pretend they don't exist. But I will learn, slowly, to keep them in that bottle.

Someone, one day, will manage to steal the top of the bottle from me. And when that happens, he or she will read my thoughts and be overwhelmed, exactly how I am right now, if not more. And he or she will know how I feel, have felt for days, and will probably feel for longer than I can possibly predict. Will my reader feel the same then?

Someone, one day, will read and understand my thoughts. Or probably he'll misunderstand them, confusing them with the stains on an old bottle, one that has been hidden in a basement for years. Or he or she will confuse my thoughts with cobwebs, or with the lack of imagination or ingenuity of the times I live in. And someone else will think I don't have thoughts at all.

But I have made up my mind. I'll learn to play this game. It's odd, slow, and complex. But I will learn it.

Today someone asked me if I was happy. A pretty legitimate question for those who play like I do.

So that was me after William. And I had predicted it well. I was still playing that game, but I was tired, and I wanted myself back. I missed him.

I turned another page of my journal. I had written about one deep exchange with him, one that had managed to pierce our silence, but only momentarily. It was months after that Christmas.

My text:

Do you ever ask yourself why we constantly look for each other? And if you ask that question, what answer do you give yourself? I'm attracted to you. My body and mind is.

His reply:

We're similar, very similar. That's why we keep looking for each other. Our friendship is beautiful and will last forever. Our attraction is complicated, though. Too complicated to manage. I miss you, but I'll let you decide if you want to continue this or not.

This had been our last, meaningful exchange. I had copied it in my journal, maybe fearing I could re-write the story one day, to feel better or worse about it, and then forget it.

I never responded to him, but I often thought about possible answers. And I wrote this one. But I never sent it.

What is that you want to continue? We're magnets. The closer you get to me, the closer I get to you, the closer you get to me. Maybe if I go far away, I'll stop hearing your voice calling me. It seems that further is never far enough, as you keep calling me. I can still hear you from here. You say you want me to be your best friend. But I don't believe you. You just feel more comfortable with me having that role. I don't.

I never sent these thoughts to William and he kept looking for me. He texted me from time to time, and kept sending me a text each Christmas. I usually didn't reply to those texts, and even when I did, my replies were terse and disinterested, almost empty. This Christmas I had not replied. I missed him though.

I grabbed my Blackberry, thought about words I could use, played with possible answers, and finally sent him an email.

Hey,

I got your Christmas text. Many things happened to me in the last few days and now I'm leaving for Italy. I might spend six months or more in Siena. I've work to do there. It's for my firm. I hope we'll talk soon, or maybe meet in Italy, or here in L.A. when I come back. Perhaps both of us made mistakes, but I'm no longer sure those mistakes are big enough to ruin our friendship. I miss my best friend.

I really did. I realized I had lost someone I loved. Call it friendship, call it something else. Perhaps there was no name for it. In any event, it didn't matter now, as I missed him, and that was all I knew.

Did Joe remind me of William? Was I trying to forgive William or Joe? Whom did I miss the most? In the good old times, I would have asked William those questions, but he wasn't there.

I felt William's arms around me, imagined us exhausted after hours of chatting about life and feelings, and drained with my losses and absences, I finally slept.

I woke up before the alarm went off. My journals were still open on my coffee table, one on top of the other.

I took a shower, got dressed, and then looked at my memories, unsure whether I should take them with me. I finally placed them in my suitcase and closed it. I looked at my graduation ring and the Prada shoe on the kitchen table, but decided to leave them there.

When I closed the door behind me I felt I was not going to return any time soon, but I had no idea what that truly meant.

A couple of hours later, I was on a flight to Italy.

9

The apartment Carla found for me in Siena was small but comfortable. It had one bedroom with a window that overlooked an alley and from which you could clearly see other apartments and their interiors. The streets were so small!

There was an ample kitchen with a marble cooking counter next to the stove. And in the living room, a simple, wood table with four chairs, and two small sofas with white matching covers.

I also had a balcony with vases of healthy and colorful flowers and plants. Someone must have tended to them, I thought, and looked around for traces of that person. There was indeed some sugar left in a glass jar, a box of cookies, an unopened pack of spaghetti. So yes, someone must have lived there before me and he or she did take good care of the apartment. I was inheriting that persons' place. Would I inherit his or her story too?

The due diligence room was about twenty minutes by car from my apartment, so each day I would take a taxi for the trip there and back.

William had replied to my email with a short, sweet one.

I have missed you too and would love to see you again. I always wanted to go to Italy, and now that you're there, I won't wait any longer. I'll plan a trip sometime before you leave and let you know. Your email made my day.

A day later, as I was thinking about that email in the due diligence room, I heard someone calling my name with a clear Italian accent. I turned and saw two young women and a young man, perhaps in their early twenties. They introduced themselves with big smiles. Chiara, Francesca, and Stefano. My team from the Milan law firm. They were friendly and welcoming and spoke perfect English. I told them I wanted to practice my Italian, but as soon as they switched to Italian, it was clear to me, and to them, that I was in over my head. So I gave up.

There was no time to waste. Simi was about to sell what appeared to be one of its more profitable subsidiaries. We had to evaluate the subsidiary, its assets and liabilities, and inform Adam and Elizabeth so they could advise Downing on whether to make an offer to buy the subsidiary or find a way to stop the sale.

I worked night and day to prepare my report, and rarely saw the sun other than when I left my apartment at sunrise. I met with people from Simi, examined volumes of financials, worked closely with my Italian team, ate pizzas and sandwiches in that due diligence room together with them and, often, with the cleaning people who would come at around midnight.

At times, the due diligence room felt like an iron box, with a heavy, low ceiling that could almost touch my brain, and no windows to escape. But if I closed my eyes, sometimes I could escape. I saw Joe and the first time we made love. And I imagined he could see me and see my memories. My escapes were brief but kept me going.

I remember writing that report while having all sorts of doubts in my mind, but doing more than my best to clear them out. I re-interviewed some of the principals, talked with them over the phone and in person, did my own investigation of Simi and its subsidiary, contacted an expert on the market and companies producing software like Simi, and even did my own investigation through an insider I was secretly introduced to by one of Stefano's friends. The amount of information I had to digest and process quickly was beyond imagination. But I made it. When I typed the last page of my report I felt a deep sense of pride and accomplishment.

I sent my report to Adam and Elizabeth and recommended prompt action. I thought the deal was going to be very profitable and I suggested that we make an offer to buy the subsidiary. Then I shut down my computer, and decided to reward myself with a good meal.

Chiara had recommended a restaurant she loved. I called a taxi and asked the driver to take me there, "Piazza del Mercato, 6." I wasn't sure I had pronounced the address properly. The driver did not ask me to repeat it, and I was worried that he had not understood me and that he would take me somewhere else. So I repeated the address and asked him if that was clear.

"Ha capito?"

"Sì, certo signorina, *Trattoria Papei*."

I checked the piece of paper Chiara had given me and the driver had it right. "*Trattoria Papei*, Piazza del Mercato, 6." This is what she wrote.

When we arrived at the restaurant, I paid and gave him a big tip. He smiled, surprised. I had forgotten that in Italy no one tips. Oh well, he seemed happy about it, and I was in the mood for celebrating. I didn't need anyone to tell me that I had done a good job. I knew I had. And I thanked the driver.

When I opened the door of the car, I forgot about the notes and documents I had kept on my knees during that short trip. When I stood up, they fell on the bricks of the square. I laughed, collected them one-by-one, and looked up.

The restaurant was, as its name indicated, a *trattoria*, a casual restaurant with great food and fair prices. In the Italian movies I had seen, trattorias looked like that one, and had tablecloths with white and red checks. My memories almost matched that place or that place my memories. What if I were now living one of those movies? I always wanted that.

My *trattoria* was on the ground floor of an old building. Its façade was romantic, with colorful laundry hanging from its balconies, and fresh lavender scent that almost perfectly blended with an intense aroma of *ragù*. I felt at home.

A brown canopy protected the patio from the sun, and beneath it, the tables seemed to be playing hide-and-seek with flowers and plants, creating a fun sense of privacy. The tablecloths were actually white.

"Quanti siete?"

"Just me."

The waitress smiled and asked me where I wanted to sit. I said outside, and pointed to a table that was the furthest back from the entrance, remote from the rest, as this is where I wanted to be and celebrate. I just needed some wine, and it'd be perfect.

As I sat and waited for my waitress to return and take my order, I looked around.

There were mainly couples, but also a group of guys celebrating something, a birthday perhaps. A street musician nearby was playing and singing beautiful Italian songs. I looked at his guitar, his fingers dancing on the strings, and I lost myself somewhere between them.

It was a night in early January, but its warmth and the laundry's lavender disoriented me. If someone had asked me what time it was, I would have probably said spring. Or late summertime.

I took off my coat, leaned back in my chair, and relaxed.

The waitress returned with a list of wines and, without even checking it, I ordered *Chianti* and "*pici al ragù*."

"A classic," the waiter said, approving my choice.

I smiled, and for a second stepped back from myself and watched my own movie, the one I had decided to be part of. I was alone, in a city I didn't know, in a country whose language was not my own, and I felt happy.

The *pici* were fabulous, and I had not eaten all day, so they soon disappeared. I stared at my clean plate and let my thoughts wander.

There was a little more to do on the project, but I wasn't in charge of drafting the offer to Simi. Other colleagues in the L.A. office were. Thus, for now, my role was largely over and I merely had to await further instructions from the firm.

So meantime what? Should I go back to L.A.? I had just started living my movie, and I was enjoying it. Going back and returning to Italy now might complicate things again, and I wasn't ready. My thoughts became bitter all of a sudden, so I thought I should order a dessert, but then decided to create my own. That would probably make the sweetness last longer.

I paid for my meal, walked to a bookstore where I could buy a recipe book, and then to a market to get the ingredients for whatever dessert I might be inspired to make. A few hours later, I was home with the book and two bags filled with possibilities.

I emptied the shopping bags and spread my purchases on the table. I opened the recipe book to the dessert section and skimmed the various options. And there it was, "*torta doppio cioccolato e arancia.*" I had all the ingredients for that. Flour, an orange, eggs, sugar, honey, cocoa, milk, whipped cream. I followed the instructions carefully and, right after 1 a.m., my cake was ready. All I needed was some coffee.

Before coming to Siena, I had never made coffee in a moka. The only "mocha" I knew was a type of coffee I could order in the U.S. that had chocolate in it and tasted like a premade beverage with cocoa powder and who knows what. The coffee I made with this *moka* was coffee.

The moka made a distinct sound as it brewed the coffee, like a tiny engine whose steam jet becomes more and more assertive as more and more coffee rises through the little holes inside of it, waiting to be savored. I grew to love the ritual of pouring water and coffee into the bottom of the moka, measuring the quantities carefully, closing the machine, placing it on the gas stove, and waiting for the sound to alert me that my ritual had worked again, and that the coffee was ready. I loved the smell of coffee rising from the machine and slowly inundating the room. I did this ritual in the morning, with my eyes still half-closed. Never at night. But that night was different. I felt I needed a bit of coffee for the cake and would not have too much, just a bit to intensify the chocolate flavor.

I cut a slice of the cake, poured a small cup of coffee, and sat on the red bricks of my balcony, my legs dangling out the railing.

As I was sipping the cake and the coffee, I saw a distinguished, older gentleman, wrapped in a long brown coat, walking down the alley. His face was partly covered by a gray hat and looked somehow familiar. The street was silent and so I think he heard my fork on the plate and looked up.

My apartment was on what Italians call the first floor—the floor above the ground floor. I moved the plants a little to see him more clearly and when I did, I smiled at him as if he had just caught me doing something I should not be doing. He smiled back, tipped his hat, and bowed politely. I followed him with my eyes and saw that he entered the door of the building next to mine.

I placed the plate in the sink, brushed my teeth, and went to make sure the window of my bedroom was closed before going to bed.

As I did, I looked to the next building and saw someone in the apartment directly across from mine, in fact the gentleman I had seen just a few minutes before on the street. He was seated at a desk, playing with what seemed to be an old camera. He was studying something, examining it carefully, and moving things around, documents, or maybe photographs given the camera.

His apartment was lit only by a dim desk lamp. I wondered if he lived alone. He seemed sweet, a man in his eighties I thought. My window was open. I closed it and went to bed.

10

The next day, I had a conference call with Adam and Elizabeth. They told me that a group in the corporate department had reviewed my report and disagreed with my conclusions. I listened carefully, explained my views, and answered their questions. They seemed satisfied and said they would get back to me.

I spent the morning cleaning the apartment and reading some magazines I'd bought the night before at the market. Then, after lunch, I decided to go for a walk to see Siena in the daylight and get a cup of coffee somewhere. It was a warm afternoon, and there were people everywhere. Mostly young. Siena was famous for its university, so I thought they might be college students. But I also saw kids with their school backpacks, some holding their mother's hand.

I walked through alleys and streets, stopped in front of bakeries and little shops, cafés, and then arrived in *Piazza del Campo*, a big square that seemed to be the focal point of the entire city. It dated from the fourteenth century, and had been paved in a fishbone-pattern of red brick. At its edge there were the *Palazzo Pubblico* and the *Torre del Mangia*, both probably from the same era as the *Piazza*. The sun shining on the *Palazzo* and the *Torre* made them look bright, almost orange brushes against the blue sky.

There were artists working on their paintings, people sitting in circles here and there, others sitting at the restaurants around the piazza, and some even lying on the bricks, as if the bricks were soft sand on which to rest and enjoy the sun.

I had again the feeling of watching an Italian movie, my movie, and felt I had to be part of it. So I decided to have coffee in that piazza and melt with it.

As I sat reading my Tuscany travel guide, I saw the old gentleman I had seen the night before, the one who lived in the apartment across from mine. He was taking photographs with an old camera, perhaps the one I had seen the night before in his apartment. He was definitely in his eighties, a bit round in the belly, carefree. He seemed from another time. Perhaps the fifties. He had thick gray hair and unattended eyebrows that obscured his small but vivid eyes. He wore gray suit pants, a white shirt with rolled up sleeves, and worn, black braces holding the pants a little higher than one would normally expect. As he took his pictures, he pressed his right eye to the viewfinder. That looked painful, but he seemed not to care. He was wandering through the piazza without any specific program, or at least none that I could see. He seemed to be taking random photos, sometimes going on the hard bricks on his knees, again not caring about them or his pants. He was trying to capture the beauty staged in his presence, almost genuflecting before it, a witness to its miracles. I thought he should be part of my movie, or he thought I should be part of his, as when he saw that I was watching him he approached me.

"*Buon giorno signorina. Le dispiace se le faccio una foto*?"

Was I part of that beauty? I was happy he had decided to photograph me because I really wanted to talk to him.

"Not at all...if you agree to join me for coffee."

My Italian was improving fast, surprisingly fast, and I hoped to become fluent soon. But I didn't feel comfortable with it yet, and I thought I should start our conversation in English to confess to him that I wasn't Italian, hoping that would not shut his interest. And it didn't, as he accepted my offer as I had accepted his, and he took several photos of me before joining me at the table.

He did not ask me to move or smile for him. He just kept moving around me, clicking his shutter, and trying to capture my different expressions, playing with the light and the shade.

I could see his camera better now that he was closer. Yes, it was old, certainly not digital. I wondered which of the photos he was taking he would actually develop, and for what purpose.

As soon as he was done, he sat at the table with me and ordered a coffee.

"This is on me." His English was perfect, definitely better than my Italian.

"Oh, no, no need," I said, trying to be friendly.

"Please," he insisted. "I owe you something. For the photos, I mean. I'm Mario, by the way."

"Clara."

We shook hands.

"Are you a professional photographer?" I asked.

"No, no. I'm...I was a teacher. I taught English at the elementary school for a long time. Then I retired, and now I take photographs for fun."

"Where did you learn English?"

"In America. My parents brought me there when I was a child. We lived in Brooklyn and then, after the war, I decided to return to Italy and become a teacher, a *maestro*, as they say here."

He smiled and sipped his espresso.

"My father's a teacher too," I said. "He teaches in college."

"I see. Are you also a teacher?"

"No, I'm a lawyer."

"A lawyer?"

Of course his reaction wasn't new to me.

"Yes, a lawyer. I know I don't look like one."

He didn't comment on that and instead asked what had brought me to Siena.

"My job. I might be here for a while."

"You'll love Siena. It's a magic city."

"Yes, I've started to believe so."

"Where are you staying?" he asked.

"Close. In *Via Banchi di sopra*, 14."

"Really? Such a small world...well, I guess Siena is small. We are neighbors. My apartment is in *Banchi di Sopra* 16."

I wanted to tell him that it was me on the balcony the night before, and that I thought I had seen him in his apartment, but I felt that was inappropriate, so I didn't mention it. However, I did say that I'd love to get together for coffee and cake perhaps. I told him I had just started baking, that I had made what I thought was a wonderful chocolate cake, that I wanted to bake more and improve, and that I let me know how I was doing. He smiled and said he thought he was qualified for that. But if we were going to share my cakes, he insisted that we share his photographs too. It would be a fair trade.

I said I'd love that. In fact, I said, I loved photography

and mentioned some of my favorite artists. He listened and smiled. I wondered what he thought of my taste.

We chatted some more and then walked together back home.

The lanterns on the side of the alleys had now replaced the sun, making the alleys feel warmer and homey. I did feel at home and safe, although that surprised me, as I hadn't been in Siena long enough to feel so.

I said "*ciao*" to Mario and told him I would stop at a market to buy some food for my dinner. He hugged me and left.

Yes, Mario had to be part of my movie, I thought.

If I had told my mother that I had made friends with this man in his eighties, that I might spend some time with him, and that he hugged me after we'd talked briefly at a café on our first meeting, she would have found that inappropriate and crazy. My father, on the other hand, would have laughed and found it special. I'd have agreed with him. My meeting with Mario had been special, and I was happy, as I had made my first friend in Siena.

I bought spaghetti and some fresh tomatoes, garlic, and basil for dinner, but before I began cooking, I checked my emails. There was no news from the law firm or from anyone else. The evening was still all mine.

My dinner was great, and after that, I looked for my chocolate cake and headed to the balcony to have my dessert there. I loved my balcony. The lanterns across the alley would barely illuminate it, and the plants hid most of it, so I could sit there unseen, observe people, listen to their chats, their laughs...Very rarely someone would raise his or her eyes and meet mine. When that happened, I would smile or pretend I was minding my own business, as I actually did. Most of the time.

That alley scene changed every night, and observing it was a way to focus on myself and my feelings at the end of the day, wrap everything in a silent prayer that only I could hear.

A couple had just kissed and I thought about Joe and our first kiss in the kitchen. I had not sent him an email or text since I had left. I looked for the travel-diary my father had given me for my birthday, and wrote Joe a letter that I never sent.

Dear Joe,

I was thinking of you tonight. A couple just kissed under my balcony and I thought about the night we kissed, in my apartment.

My first days here have been intense, and I didn't see much of Siena until today. It's truly beautiful. People seem happy. Their life is simple and full, joyful. I made a friend. His name is Mario, he's in his eighties, and lives in a building next to mine. He was an English teacher and takes photographs for fun. He hugged me tonight, and his hug felt good. I probably terribly needed a hug and he knew that better than I did, until he hugged me.

I have started baking and yesterday I made a wonderful double chocolate and orange cake. You might have liked it. Or maybe not. I actually don't know if you like chocolate. I do.

I reviewed my thoughts and was ready to go back inside my apartment when I saw Mario going out. I checked the time on my computer. It was almost eleven. I wondered where he could be going at that time. Maybe that was just his regular night walk. I hid behind the plants, as I didn't want him to see me and think I might be spying on him. Fortunately, he did not look up and kept walking. I wanted to wait for him, see when he would come back, but I was too tired. It had been an intense, beautiful day, and now it was time to go to bed.

11

The next morning a strong aroma of coffee woke me up. I'd been dreaming of Joe. In my dream, he had come to visit me in Siena and was making coffee in my kitchen. I opened my eyes and ran to the kitchen, but soon realized I had been dreaming. And yet I could sense the aroma of coffee. It was intense, and came from Mario's apartment. His window was open, mine was too, and so it was as if he had made it in my bedroom or, as I thought, in my kitchen. I opened the window more widely and called him.

"Mario!"

"Clara? We are so close. Why don't you come over for coffee?"

"I'm still in my pajamas."

"I'll wait, if you promise to bring a slice of that cake you mentioned yesterday."

I said it was fine, put on my jeans and a sweater, and crossed the alley to Mario's building. His apartment was on the first floor. His building almost identical to mine. Same stairway. Same doors. In fact, I felt I was climbing the stairway to my own apartment.

I knocked on the door that had a consumed bronze plate on its top. It said "Mario Pellegrini." That was surely it.

The door was half open and the aroma of coffee had swept into the hallway.

He came to the door and welcomed me into an apartment filled with books and beautiful, old furniture, with a scent of antiquity. The aroma of coffee mixed with that scent gave me the impression that I was still dreaming. I felt I had entered a black and white movie where everything appeared simple and genuine, distant from the chaos of our times. A safe zone.

The walls were entirely covered by photographs, all carefully framed, one close to another, each from a different time, with a different subject, background, light, all of them combined to make a strong artistic statement.

"Did you take these?" I asked.

"Yes, most of them. I've already processed some, but not all."

"What do you mean by 'processed'?"

"I write a story for each photo I take. The story the photo tells me, or the one the person in the photo shares with me. If I can talk to that person, as I am doing with you, if I get to know them, then my story might include some of what I've learned about them. If not, I try to see the story in their eyes, the way they dress, how they are placed within the world of the photograph...."

"Have you written many stories?" I asked, feeling that I was about to discover a treasure.

"Oh, yes. Many."

"Can I read them?"

He smiled.

Had I asked too much?

"Of course. Please, sit." He pointed to his kitchen table, and soon came back with two cups of espresso and the chocolate cake I had brought. His coffee and my cake were perfect together.

"Your cake is delicious," he said, finishing the last bite.

"I'm only learning to bake."

"It seems you're learning well. Come with me."

He took me to a large cardboard box that looked like a paper footlocker. He opened it, and inside was a neatly organized filing system, hundreds of separate files. He explained that each file contained a photograph, and one hundred fifty-three of the files also contained a story he had written for that photo.

"I have many more stories to write, but my hands slow me down." He held out his hands to show me his fingers misshapen by arthritis.

"You write the stories by hand?"

"Is there another way?" He smiled.

He took out one of the files and handed it to me. It contained a photograph of a woman in her late twenties. She was leaning out the window of a car to check her lipstick in that car's mirror. He must have taken that photo sometime in the 60s, I thought, as her clothes and hairstyle seemed from that time. The photo was a close-up of the woman, and you could barely see the car. But from what I saw, the car seemed from that same era. And the file also contained a twenty-page handwritten story. *Luna* was its title. I asked if Luna was also the name of the woman in the photograph, and he nodded. He said he did not know her, that he had taken that photo while he was waiting for a friend on the side of the street where the car was parked. I thought the picture perfectly captured the idea of that woman and her times. A lady checking her makeup in the mirror of a car and expressing her full self in the split second it took to click the shutter.

Mario was an artist.

"What made you take this photograph?" I asked.

"I don't know. I saw something, and so, click." And he mimed taking a picture of me.

We looked at several more photographs. A group of old men playing cards on a newspaper rack. A mother kissing her baby on his forehead. A distinguished man lost in his thoughts. A couple looking into each other's eyes after they had just kissed. An elderly woman dressed in black and clutching a rosary in her hands. Those subjects revealed secrets about themselves, their feelings, their innermost thoughts. And perhaps, in one way or another, they spoke about Mario too. I could easily understand how he would feel inspired to give those photos a voice, the narrative that they themselves were telling silently.

I took a file and sat on Mario's sofa.

"Can I read this one?"

The file's title was "*Cha-cha for Lovers*," and the photo showed a diverse group of people dancing cha-cha in an old-basement.

They were old and young, tall and short, elegant and awkward, somber and light hearted. I thought such a group would hardly blend. But maybe I was wrong, and so I skimmed Mario's story to find out. A line said that those students had fallen in love. Most of them with one another. And most of them after joining the school. So there must be something about that school that made love happen.

I smiled and returned to the photo, to see if I could spot the lovers. Were they the ones dancing or chatting around the dancing floor? Was that so obvious? I looked at them and thought that couldn't be true. They really looked too different from one another. And who was the teacher? Had she fallen in love with one of her students too? I took Mario's file and started reading.

The teacher's name was Marisol. She was tall, had long, blond hair, and wore an open shoulder, light pink dress that almost matched her lipstick. I couldn't see that from the photo, as the photo was in black and white, but I thought a light pink would match her eyes and her smile. And true, I didn't know who Marisol was when I had first looked at that photo, but now that I thought about it, I wondered how could I have possibly missed her. She stood to the side, somewhat aloof from the dancers. Her posture was a model of perfection. The posture of a ballerina, proud of her art, aware of her elegance.

Mario's story described Marisol only briefly, her solitude, her silences, and how well she covered a sadness that would have been out of place in that room. He said she had fallen in love. But no, it wasn't one of her students. I wished Mario had said more.

And then the story zoomed in on each couple, sometimes offering curious details. It talked about the high school teacher with rounded black glasses dancing with a check-out assistant, who was almost always wearing her uniform. The older post-grad student who danced with his classmate, perhaps ten years younger and 3 feet shorter. The engineer always carrying a compass in his pocket protector, to draw perfect circles. He danced with the custodian who perhaps had erased the circles the students had drawn on the chalk boards. And then there was the professional sumo wrestler dancing with the English teacher.

Mario heard me laugh as I read about them. I turned and saw him smiling. I wondered if he remembered what he had written.

The wrestler was silent but mostly smiling. And the teacher loved to talk, but was mainly sad. One would have said that opposites attract, but Mario thought that they were actually more similar than they appeared. If you only looked deeper into their eyes you would see that. I took the photo and checked their eyes. As I was trying to see what he had described, Mario came closer to take one of his books from the shelves and I lost focus. I thought about asking him what he had seen in that couple's eyes but before I did, he had already returned to his office, probably thinking that I should be walking inside those photos and their stories on my own.

I spent some more time on the cha-cha file, and then pulled the file of the little store that sold secrets. *The Secrets Shop.*

The photo showed a woman in her store. She was round-shouldered and almost consumed by the past, hers or her customers'. The store was tucked in an alley and it sold secrets. The woman would buy artifacts from anyone who could convince her that the artifact contained a secret. She would not ask them to explain what the secret was and how to find it. But they had to convince her that they were selling her the opportunity of a journey. And if they did so and she bought it, she would give them *cinque lire*. "*Cinque lire a segreto*," this is what the chalk board said at the entrance of her store.

I wandered inside the photo and its shelves. I saw little jars, a beautiful hairbrush, a tiny, consumed book, a musical ballerina jewelry box whose carillon I could almost hear, a tin train with a missing car, a boy who looked like a doll or a doll that looked like a boy with a nice sailor hat and big eyes, a folded paper or letter or song or poetry, an empty envelope, an hourglass, a lantern with a broken bulb, an empty bottle, a full one, one with a ship in it. The photo was filled with stories all pushing to come to life like the toys in the fight scene of *The Nutcracker*. I wondered if they would do that when I closed the file.

"Do you like them?" Mario then asked, returning with two cups of fresh coffee.

"I'm speechless," I said, and I was, speechless in that little refuge of magic, toys, dreams, and secrets. I looked around trying to understand where I really was, and then asked him about the two stories I had just read. I wanted to know if they were true.

"What do you think?"

"I don't know. They seem true."

He took the files in his hands, leafed through the pages, but didn't confirm that. Maybe he no longer remembered, I thought.

"Why do you write these stories?"

"What else would I do?" He smiled and handed the files back to me.

"What do you mean?" I asked, wondering whether my question had been too personal. But then he explained.

"When I was younger it was hard to make friends, to open myself to people. In America, I was too Italian and in Italy, at least when I first came back, I was too American.

"After many years, I finally made my first real friend, and he remained my only one. I wish I had made more friends like him, but perhaps that's not possible.

"I took photographs before meeting him, but when I lost

him, photography became my obsession. And the photographs started talking to me, and I started writing their stories."

"What was your friend's name?"

"Gianni."

Mario looked sad, lost somewhere, no longer with me, not in that room. So I tried to pull him back into his nicer memories.

"These stories are beautiful. And the photos. You should collect them in a book and consider publishing it," I said, but he remained silent, and continued to look at the photos on the wall.

He seemed again lost in his memories, but this time I couldn't say if they were happy or sad. Whatever he was thinking, though, whatever memories those photos were triggering, I thought he ought to be aware of their artistic value, their potential.

"I'm not a professional, Clara. I do this from the heart. Plus, my stories are handwritten and not many people would want to read my handwriting."

"I can read it," I said, "and I could type them on my computer. I type fast and you could dictate them to me, if necessary."

"You are too kind, but I don't think this would be a good idea. You are a busy lawyer."

"I insist. I'd really love to do that together."

"How will I compensate you?"

"With your friendship?"

I checked the time and it was nine. I had to run home, check my emails, and see whether there was any further instruction from the firm. I thanked Mario, hugged him, and left.

When I got home, I found an email from Elizabeth, who

had copied Adam and my Italian team.

Clara,

We have thoroughly reviewed your report and agree with your assessment. We have advised Downing to act according to your proposal and assume the risks that the corporate department presented to us. He agrees. We have sent a tentative offer to Simi and it's possible we'll have to negotiate the terms of the offer. I'll talk to you as soon as I hear back from Simi's CEO. Thanks again for your hard work and commitment to this. The client and the other partners truly appreciate it.

Best,

Elizabeth

That email made me happy, and made me feel like I deserved a reward, more time for myself, work-free. I went back to my bedroom, called Mario, and asked him if I could pick up a few of his files.

"I think I might have a day or two off, and I'd love to start working on our project."

"You said you haven't seen much of Siena, though. I'll give you the files if you let me give you a tour of the city. Maybe later today or tomorrow?"

I agreed, returned to Mario's place, got twenty of his files, and went back to my apartment excited, looking forward to studying the photos and reading their stories.

I placed the files on the floor, fanning them out, I ran my fingers across them, and then picked one at random.

I studied the photo for a while, and tried to imagine a story for it. It showed a woman holding a little boy's hand. The boy wore a school backpack, and was pointing his feet toward the street, trying to resist his mother's grip. He was probably going to school.

In my story, the one I would have written, the mother was happy to be taking her son to school. She would have a few hours for herself, maybe would take a walk or go to a café where she would meet her friends. The boy loved being with her. Earlier that morning, she had read him a fairy tale from a big book showing giant elephants flying in the sky among clouds made of cotton candy. He wanted more of that. She told him that they would have cotton candy that afternoon if he went to school with a smile.

I could have continued imagining and imagining, but I was too curious to read what Mario had seen.

The story was thirty-two pages long and with very few corrections, two words he had deleted, two or three he had added. Did he write drafts of each story before writing a final, clean version? That would have taken forever. Could he see the entire story before writing it?

In Mario's story the woman's name was "Delia," and the title of the story was *Delia's Secret Life*. She was taking Dario, her little boy, to school. Dario was six and in first grade. He was holding a plastic car in his hand. I had missed that car when I looked at the photo. The car was a gift his father had given him just before kissing him goodbye earlier. Delia was in her forties. She had married twice and she had Dario from her second marriage. She wasn't happy. She had big dreams, had hoped to become an actress one day, but got married when she was too young, and now had four kids.

Delia's second husband, Ferdinando, was a bit older than she. He was a banker, rarely at home, and rarely spent time with her. He was pragmatic, believed in money, and discouraged Delia from pursuing any artistic career. Soon after the wedding, Delia realized that she had made a mistake but she was already pregnant with Dario, so she thought she should stay in the new relationship for the baby and the other three kids, and do her best to make it work.

Once Dario was old enough to go to the kindergarten,

she secretly joined a theatre company. She loved acting, and approached each role she played, no matter how small, with full artistic commitment. She was superb in the role of Filumena in *Filumena Marturano*, a Neapolitan play in which the main character, Filumena, is a former prostitute who married, repeatedly cheated on her husband, and had three children, only one of whom was her husband's. Mario's description of Delia's dreams and her conflicts with Ferdinando made them seem real. Did he really make up that story? Did he know Delia? Would he tell me?

I made more tea, found a radio station playing jazz from the 20s, and went to the balcony to take a break from the reading.

I loved Mario and his artistic spirit. I wondered whether all Italians were like him, and I thought that even if I had stopped playing, my heart was still that of an artist.

I started looking at the people passing below my balcony, and slowly the jazz wrapped the entire scene in a bygone time. It was early afternoon. Some of those people were probably leaving their offices for lunch. Others were heading home from school or from a trip to the market. I took photos of them in my head and imagined their stories, the ones Mario might have written. That exercise exhausted me and so I decided to take a nap. Before I did, though, I wrote more in my diary.

Dear Joe,

Mario showed me his collection of photos today. He writes stories about the people he photographs. He handwrites them, and they seem real. I asked him if they were, but he didn't answer. Perhaps I asked the wrong question, as there are no truths to be found in those stories, just journeys to take.

The radio is playing jazz from the 20s. I feel you would like this one. I think I might have met you and found you through your music. I wished I had thought about that before.

The window of my room was open. The air was warm, the music was still playing, and they both lullabied me to sleep.

12

That afternoon and for several days after I explored the city with Mario. He knew all the hidden and secret places of Siena that I would have never discovered on my own, or at least not as I did with him. We saw buildings, towers, churches, fountains. All from another time that he seemed to know so well. And we walked everywhere, tried different trattorias, but often returned to *Trattoria Papei*, out favorite.

In view of our offer, Simi had agreed not to sell the subsidiary and my job had slowly become less and less demanding, and that was a relief, as I was more and more tired and distracted. And perhaps less interested too.

Chiara, Francesca, and Stefano had completed their assignments and I was on my own. I actually enjoyed that too. I could have easily returned to L.A., stayed a week or two and then returned to Siena. But I was enjoying Siena too much, and I didn't want to leave. Plus, returning to L.A. would mean facing Joe and I wasn't ready for that either.

Mario and I were becoming closer each day. We talked

about us, our points of view, tastes, ideas, love. I told him about William. And I told him about Joe and my feelings for him. He said he understood. He really seemed to. I had long thought that Mario must have loved someone deeply, so I wasn't surprised when he said that he had, but I wanted to know more.

"Who was she?" I asked.

He looked down,

"*He*... Gianni," he said and looked away.

I went closer to him, and put my hand over his.

"Do you want to talk about him?"

And so Gianni lived again. For me and for him. And I could see Mario more clearly.

He told me how they met, how Mario feared his feelings for him, how he tried to hide them, and how he eventually hid their relationship from others, while Gianni wanted it to be open. Mario was afraid he might lose his job or be treated harshly, and he was concerned for Gianni too.

"This was a different time, you know?" he said, and seemed to be looking for my mercy or his own.

He and Gianni stayed together for over fifteen years, until Gianni died. And then Mario realized he had lost his only chance to love, but there was no more time for that.

The following days love became our main theme. Sometimes the only one. Mario knew much more than I did, and I listened.

"You need to know yourself deeply to fall in love with someone."

He was right. Did I know myself well enough to fall in love?

Time started to fly.

Every day I woke up with the sunrise, made my coffee,

and worked on Mario's stories. Sometimes we reviewed the stories the evening before I would begin typing. I would go to his place after work and we would spend the night on the files and their stories. Sometimes I would bring pizza, others he would make pasta. And we would talk for hours about the photo and the story before working on it. Or we would not talk about the story at all before typing it. But I always had questions for him, sometimes moving beyond the story, deeper into his memories, his feelings or mine. And often his stories too expanded beyond their pages, sometimes trespassing into traditions, recipes, movies. I was travelling throughout Italy with him, and yet we were still seated in his living room most of the time.

I read and typed the story of an actor who lost his job and decided to open his own theatre and teach acting to children. The story of a violinist who, after a trauma, could only express himself through his music. The story of the scientist who was studying immortality and kept falling in love with younger women. The story of a painter who fell in love with his painting.

The details of those stories were so rich that I was almost always sure they were real. And I had not discarded the idea that those stories were like journeys, but sometimes I needed to believe that those journeys were real, and I was disappointed when, sometimes after working on them, Mario would reveal the contrary.

"You see, Clara. You believe that these stories are real because each photo tells you precisely the story I have written for them. If you look at the photo carefully without missing any detail, you'll find the story I have told or a similar one. I'm just being faithful to the photographs, that's all."

He was right. Those photos told unfiltered stories. And whenever I stopped and thought about possibilities for any of them, my ideas were never that distant from Mario's, and they became increasingly similar to his the closer I looked and the closer we got to each other.

"I don't think it's just beauty you're looking for," I said one day, studying one of his photos. "You're looking for yourself, aren't you?"

"Yes. That must be true. What else does one look for?"

Yes, we were getting closer.

My time with Mario was magic. We both liked the music of the 20s and 30s, and loved jazz from that time. Mario had a huge collection of albums and we listened to them on his old gramophone, drinking his red wines, and eating my cakes. I was experimenting, looking for things, into things. We both were.

Mario explained to me that he usually wrote his stories in one sitting, making only a few corrections or additions each time. So he did see the story, all of it, before writing it. Mario was poetry. Everything about him was.

Often, while I was typing, he would come closer, offer me his right hand, and drag me into the middle of the living room to dance to a jazz arrangement. I loved dancing with him. He made me feel light, and he made me laugh. Oh, God, if we laughed.

"You see, you can't resist the music," he would say, looking at me with his eyes half closed, but filled with passion.

We danced, and talked, and wrote, and danced more. He was a wonderful dancer and taught me some nice moves. Sometimes I fell down, or tripped over his feet, and then we would laugh and continue dancing until we were exhausted.

I did see my movie. I was at its center. And there was Mario, his photos, his stories, the paintings, the wine, the food, the jazz from the 20s. They were all dancing around me, with me, around and around. We were melting.

And the months were melting too, so when June came, with its colors and flavors, claiming its identity, it almost caught me by surprise. I opened the windows and balcony wide, and June entered, day after day, and slowly took over. The scent of jasmine was everywhere. Sometimes even in my cakes or in my bathtub water. I hadn't even looked for jasmine this time. She had found me, and it was real.

My heart was beating for life and its beauty, and when I paused to look inside of me, I felt happy. I missed Joe, but felt I had a long way to go before he could meet the person I wanted him to meet. Jasmine had just found me. I was leaving my silences, but some of them were still there, stuck in my heart.

William had been the first to pull me from my music. He was the only one I could talk to besides my piano. And in fact, I hadn't talked much with him either. I mainly listened to his stories, and helped him decide what to do, sometimes when he had already decided. Or I helped him pick among options, sometimes when he had one choice only, but he didn't know or didn't want to know.

I would write him long letters. He preferred the telephone. He would call and keep me on the phone for hours. I hated talking on the phone, and told him so, but he forgot, or pretended that he had. Our phone calls could last hours. And during those calls, sometimes he would manage to crack one of my silences, and I then surprised him. Or perhaps I didn't, as he knew me well, he knew my heart, and my confessions were truths he just wanted me to hear.

We were similar. He often said so. But he loved to plan everything. I could just improvise. When I told him that once, he said there was a plan behind improvisation too, and it was so perfect that I could not even see it. I disagreed with him on that. Improvisation and its plan, assuming there was any, to me were nature's perfection.

But agreeing or disagreeing with him wasn't the point. I loved talking with him. More than with anyone else. Talking with him was like playing my piano, it tasted like jasmine. This is how I had fallen in love with him. Had I really? And what about him? He would have never told me. He had planned my role in his life. I was going to be his best friend. For life. It would work like this. And he was probably right. But what about my feelings? I didn't, couldn't plan them.

When we, when I stopped talking with William, I lost that jasmine and myself, somewhere in my silences. But now jasmine had found me, I had found Mario. My heart was learning to talk again, it was beating loud again. Mario's stories my heart's sounding board. And the sound slowly became louder and louder. I was alive again.

I had already read and typed thirty of Mario's stories when I found the file that changed the course of the events.

It was June 27. That day Mario and I met for breakfast to share a pie I had baked and a story I had typed. The story was beautifully written. I thought it didn't need any editing. I re-read it once to him, he approved it, and we toasted with coffee.

Then he left the room and came back with another file. As he handed it to me, we continued chatting about a movie we saw, an independent film we were trying to decipher without success. Then I checked the time, called a taxi, and went to work.

As I was in the taxi, I opened the file and saw a photo of...me.

"*Signorina, siamo arrivati.... Signorina?*"

"*Oh, sì, scusi. Ecco.*"

I paid the driver and got out of the taxi. My legs barely supporting me.

I rushed into the due diligence room, placed my bag on the desk, and the file on top of it. I looked at the photo again. Like many of Mario's photographs, this one was in black and white and seemed to be from thirty or so years ago. I closed the door to my office, and pulled the photograph and the story from the file. *Looking for Clara*. Did she have my name too?

The woman in the photo was thin, my height, and in her late twenties or early thirties. She was serving pastries in a bakery. I pushed my eyes deeper into me, but when I opened them again, she was still there, and that title too.

She had long blond hair and big eyes. I couldn't see their color, but they seemed bright and sad. She was not wearing makeup, but her skin was luminous and her lips reflected an intense red, one that was almost piercing the black and white patina of the photograph. She was wearing a tight three-quarter sleeve shirt and what appeared to be a soft, ample skirt mostly hidden by a small counter and its pastries and cakes. She was smiling, but her smile was not full, almost clouded by her eyes' veil of sadness.

It was me in that photo. Was I in her story too? Mario had written *Looking for Clara* in the first person. He had not used the first person for any other story I had read. Was this one real?

I turned the page and read the first lines.

I had the pleasure of knowing a lovely woman named Clara. She was a simple, elegant creature, of a rare beauty, a beauty that grows from within. Her voice was music and when she walked she seemed to dance.

When Mario met Clara she was thirty-one. He had just turned fifty.

Clara was a baker. She owned a café in an alley leading to *Piazza Salimbeni*, close to *Via Banchi di Sopra*. *Caffé Siena*. Mario discovered her café on a summer afternoon, while wandering the streets and alleys of Siena. He had not yet met Gianni and spent much of his time alone. The simple beauty of that café called Mario in.

He entered, looked at the display of pastries, and then sat at a small table, on one of the two wrought-iron chairs. There was an intriguing design on the back of the chairs. He studied it and tried to understand what it was, if anything.

"I believe it's a heart," Clara said, interrupting the flow of his thoughts.

He raised his eyes to meet hers, smiled, and said he thought the design looked more like the hat an eccentric man would wear at a fancy party in Venezia. Maybe a violet velvet hat. She laughed.

"What a vivid imagination. You must be an artist."

"I'm just a teacher who likes to imagine," he said, and laughed with her.

When Clara said she was the baker, the one making the pastries on display, Mario asked her to suggest one he might want to try. She studied him for a while, worked the alternatives through her mind, and then recommended a *torta di mele* she had made earlier that morning.

"I think you'll enjoy it because it's simple and sophisticated, refreshing and warm. It will leave you wondering about its hidden flavors. Some of them might remind you of velvet."

Mario was sold on that one. And who would not be? A cake with a hint of velvet?

Mario described his first conversation with Clara as magic, perfect, and filled with nonsense. They immediately connected. Her and her café, somehow isolated from everything else by thick layers of love and grace, made him lose perception of time and space, and he forgot to look for the velvet ingredient. Was he supposed to do that? Did she ask him to? He could not remember.

When Clara returned to Mario's table to ask him what he thought of the cake, Mario said it was sublime. She was so happy. She explained to Mario that the "secret" ingredient, the velvet one, was licorice, and that almost nobody ever identified it. She thought the combination of licorice, apples, and *limoncello* gave a warm, velvet-like flavor to the cake. Mario agreed. They laughed at the level of sophistication they were using to describe a cake, and Mario left the café feeling so much lighter than when he had entered.

He returned to Clara's café almost every day before going to school, and sometimes on the weekends before exploring the city with his camera. It must have been on one of those occasions that he took the photo in the file that was now on my desk.

All of Clara's customers seemed to be her friends, or so Mario thought. They brought her gifts, showed her pictures of their babies or grandchildren, and paid careful attention to whatever she said. Sometimes Mario would learn about Clara just by listening to the chatter that flowed around her. Among other things, he learned that she was a pianist, that she taught piano at home to a small group of children, and that from time to time she performed in public. She preferred to play for herself or her students, though, and performed in public only when she needed money. But after she opened the café, that rarely happened.

He thought Clara was passion, but that she had not explored that passion completely. She said she wasn't sure she had ever fallen in love, but hoped she would one day. She had dreamt to be an artist. A pianist or a ballerina. But then convinced herself that she lacked talent, and so never pursued her dreams.

Clara seemed more interested in other people than in herself, and so she observed them, studied them, and seemed to understand what they needed. But Mario thought she wasn't fully aware of herself.

Why did she become a baker? How could she successfully run a public business and yet be uncomfortable performing in public? Why did she pick Siena over Firenze, the place where she was born? Why did she prefer old movies to new ones? How could she like Baudelaire and think of herself as someone resisting passionate and irrational choices? When Mario asked Clara these questions, she had no answers for him, and he felt sad for her. A flower unaware of her beauty. This is what he thought of her.

Clara thought of herself as fragile but, in fact, Mario thought she was strong and brave. She started her own business with money an aunt had left her when she died. That wasn't enough. She could have sought support from her aristocratic family, but she never did, and never used her status to achieve anything. She was beautiful and elegant, not "just a baker," as she defined herself.

Clara told Mario about her recipes, her baking experiments and discoveries, the ingredients she used and where she got them from, the places she had been to find them. She told him about the Amalfi Coast and how much she loved that area. She would go there at least once a year to buy the best *limoncello*, get some citrus and oranges, try new pastries, and find new ideas for her own. And she loved Perugia and the areas around that city.

I loved that story, but I was also a bit confused and perhaps scared, wondering about my relationship with that woman who had my name, looked like me, and seemed to have too much in common with me. Was that me in another life? Was Mario playing tricks on me? Was I doing that to myself? My movie now looked like a dream, but the dream seemed real.

Mario's story also described Clara's closest friends, and one of them at length. Verde. I loved that name. She was a romantic and dreamy actress, who lived her life as if she were always on a stage.

"Mario, this is Verde," Clara introduced her to him one day. "I'm sure she'll soon become a great movie star," she said, her eyes proud of her friend.

Clara and Verde had different personalities but were very close. Perhaps Clara saw in Verde what she wanted to be. She believed in her and never missed one of Verde's performances.

One summer, they went to Perugia, to the jazz festival. It was July. Verde fell in love with a drummer they met, and a few months later, she left Siena and moved to Perugia to live with him. When Verde left, Clara felt a sense of loss. She told Mario about it, and became sadder every day. She said she wanted to have a baby.

It was around that time that Mario met Gianni.

Mario's visits to the bakery became less and less frequent, as he was jealous of his privacy with Gianni, and worried that going public would hurt what they had.

Months later, when Mario decided to introduce Gianni to Clara, they walked to the café, but found it closed. It was a

Sunday morning. Clara might have changed her policy, he thought. The café could be now closing on Sundays. They left, but Mario returned to the café again and again. The café was always closed, and one day it was gone. Its space was empty, and workers were painting the walls, somehow preparing them for something else.

He stopped, entered, and asked those workers if they knew *Café Siena*, whether it had moved somewhere else. They didn't know. He also asked people in the neighborhood. Everyone confirmed that the café had closed without advance notice. No one knew why or where Clara had gone.

He felt guilty for having abandoned her, and worried about her. He looked for her for a while, but then there was work and Gianni, and Clara slowly vanished from Mario's life the same way she had entered. As a dream.

I turned page and found a blank one. And then on the next page, in a different ink, the story continued and explained why the café had closed.

Clara met a man on a train during one of her trips to Perugia. He was not from Siena or from Perugia. She married him but a few years later, the two separated. Clara went back to her parents' home in Firenze and started a new life there.

Really? Is this how it ended? What about the baby she wanted? Did she have that? Firenze was so close to Siena. Did he visit her there?

My Blackberry rang. It was Elizabeth. She said she had good news for me. They had received the data of the first trimester for Simi's subsidiary, and they were overwhelmingly good. Downing was thinking of buying additional companies in Italy, and he wanted me on the new projects. She said he had actually put that as a condition for him to keep doing business with the law firm. And as she said that, she laughed.

"Oh. That's good to hear," I said, but I must have sounded not that enthusiastic. I was distracted. That photo, the story.

"We might need you to stay longer in Italy."

There was a long pause, and then she spoke again.

"You must be exhausted. You haven't taken any time off since you started working for us and you've been working hard for months. You should take a vacation. What do you say?"

I said I would think about it.

I spent the rest of the day staring at pages filled with numbers and words that my question marks shaded off more and more, the more I thought about that file. I considered going home earlier, but tried to push myself to complete more work. In the afternoon, when I finally realized that my mind had left that due diligence room right after reading Clara's story, I called a taxi and returned home.

When I got there, I went to Mario's apartment, and knocked on his door.

"Clara, it's a little early for you, no? What is it?"

I looked at him without knowing where to start. I was holding Clara's file in my hands and placed it on his table. I opened it and showed him the photo.

"What do you see?" I asked.

"The file I gave you this morning?"

He scanned the photo, skimmed the pages, and then turned to me.

"It's called *Looking for Clara*," I added, my hands shaking.

"Oh...I see. And the name..."

I remained silent. Had I made my movie real?

"She really looks like you," he said, and checked the

photo once again. “I thought you reminded me of someone when we met, you looked familiar, but I couldn’t say. Clara, right. That’s really interesting.”

I needed something convincing, a story that would make sense. She wasn’t just my double. She was me. She baked, she played piano, she didn’t like playing in public, she loved Baudelaire....

“Did you meet her? Can you tell me more about her?”

“Yes and yes,” he answered, while skimming the story.

“Is the story real?”

“I think so,” he said. “I don’t remember everything, though. I’ll have to think about this.”

He went to the sofa to be alone with the file, free from my questions for a little while, trying to remember. I took the photo and sat far from him to give him space. I looked at the photo again.

Clara looked like a caring person, one that would have a best friend she wanted to protect, one who would make pastries for living and loved doing that. She could have been a pianist, her fingernails were trim. She did not have a wedding ring. She might be dreaming of falling in love and later marry.

“The story I wrote sounds right, real,” he then said. “But I’m not a hundred percent sure of all of it. Sometimes I liked to weave in ideas and details that were not part of reality. To make the story more truthful to itself, or to my idea of it. Of course I met Clara, the woman in the photo. And, yes, Clara was her name. Her personality, her job, what I say here seems right. I never introduced Gianni to Clara and I’m certain I haven’t seen her since the bakery closed. I’m not sure about the ending of that story, though. Something about it doesn’t sound right. I might have written it sometime after I wrote the story. Perhaps to give it an ending.

Now that I read it, though, this doesn't feel like its ending. Who knows what I was thinking when I wrote it?"

I took a deep breath, joined Mario on the sofa, and sank into it. Then I went to his gramophone, chose one of his jazz LPs, put it on, and asked him to dance with me.

The name of the piece was *Huggable, Kissable You*.

He hugged me and we danced.

"If this is real, I want to find her. I need to."

He didn't ask why, just promised we would.

13

When the music stopped, I asked Mario if we could visit the place where the café used to be. It was late, but he agreed to take me there. He led me down a short alley off *Via Banchi di Sopra* and then *Via dei Termini*, where he said Clara's bakery once was.

The street was narrow, an alley blowing permanence. I felt not much had changed over the years. The buildings' pinkish and grey bricks, rough in texture, evoked a medieval past. I could almost sense the scent of that time. Who knows where that perception came from? And if I closed my eyes, that silent alley suddenly filled with women and men attending to their errands, with the candor and passion I thought people from those times might have had.

Among the pinkish and greyish buildings there was a yellow one, bright and freshly painted. A modern contrast to its neighbors. That mix of bright and subdued, old and new, and the brush of sunset light, wrapped the alley, somehow protecting the dream from reality, and perhaps us too.

So this was the street Clara had chosen for her café. I would have chosen it too. I imagined her walking along *Via dei Termini* before the sun rose, ready to unlock the café, her thoughts filled with recipes and plans for the day. I pressed my eyes more inside of me. They cried for the beauty they saw. Satie was playing again.

"It was somewhere near here," Mario then said, looking around and trying to remember. But after some wandering, he stopped.

"Here. *Caffé Siena* was here."

What was once a bakery called *Caffé Siena* was now *Bar Termini*. The new owner chose a humble and circumscribed name, the name of the street instead of the city. *Bar Termini.* I thought "Siena" was better. I would have chosen that name.

Mario remained outside for a while, perhaps trying to confirm to himself that the *Bar* had truly been *Caffé Siena* once.

I entered. The small display was now a big counter that took up much of the floor space. And there were no tables, except for a small one with two chairs, pushed to the furthest back. You would almost miss it if you didn't look carefully. As I was looking around, Mario joined me, dragged by his memories.

"These are Clara's chairs," he said. "This is the table where I sat." He pointed to the backs of the chairs. "She said it was a heart. I thought it was a hat."

I could see the heart plainly.

"I'm sure this is it. The table. The chairs." We ordered two coffees and sat there.

"I wish I had come here with Gianni," he then said. "I wish she had met him." He was walking through his memories and I was there with him, holding his hand, almost part of his past, perhaps his Clara at times.

"When I was with Gianni, we tried to avoid Siena as

much as we could. The city was too small, everyone knew everyone, and I did not want people to see us together. They would have understood."

He looked around, somehow suspicious again, as if someone could join our table, uninvited, and judge him again, misunderstand him again, hurt him again. But then he realized he was safe, or perhaps decided he wasn't going to care this time, and continued.

"We often went out of town or just stayed home. And after Gianni died, I rarely went to cafés and bars. I didn't want to be on my own, sit before a drink, question myself or my past. I tried to stay distracted and whenever I had the chance, kept moving. A café is a place where you go to think, and after Gianni, I didn't want to. I didn't want to think."

He raised his eyes to meet mine, somehow asking me if I could understand, if I could see what he went through. I think I did. My heart cried.

As we sipped our coffee in silence, Mario continued to wander around the café and his memories.

"You know," he said at some point, "I think it was Clara who inspired me to write stories for my photos. I remember coming here one day and sharing with her one of my early photographs, the one of the woman checking her makeup in the car's mirror, the one you saw.

"I showed her that photograph and she loved it. You could tell when she loved something because she would smile first, a big, loud smile. And then she'd shout "*l' adoro!*" and laugh. I can still hear her laughing. Her entire being would laugh and shout her thoughts, her happiness. She was a delight to watch. I wanted to hug her whenever she did that, and I probably did. Almost always." He smiled.

Was I ever like that? Did my being ever shout myself? I

wanted that. As he continued to talk about her, I thought I wanted to be Clara.

"Clara wanted to talk about that photo, tell me what she saw in it. The woman's story. This is where I got the idea of writing my stories. She never actually said I should do that, but this is where I got the idea. I had forgotten...."

He looked at me and said,

"Thank you for bringing me here."

I was thankful too.

14

The day after, I woke up thinking of Clara. I wrote an email to Elizabeth, said I had thought about her offer and would take some time off before committing to another project. She replied right away, and I was officially on vacation.

I turned off my computer and felt free to go. Where to, though, wasn't clear.

I took Clara's story with me, left my apartment, and walked to *Piazza del Campo*. It was morning. The sun was warm, and I felt warm too. On a week day morning. People were walking to work, tourists were making plans for the day. I was just thinking.

I pulled my travel diary and listed the places in Clara's story, those where she had been, those she liked.

Siena
Firenze
Amalfi
Perugia

Would I like those places too? Would I find her there? And then I wrote "Verde" right below my list. I liked that name, and wanted to meet her too. Would we become friends?

I turned the page of my journal, and wrote to Joe. Another letter I would not send.

Dear Joe,

Time is flying. I love Siena and, at times, I feel I'm living a movie. Yesterday, in one of Mario's files, I found a photo of someone named Clara who looks so much like me. Her story is calling me in.

Mario said he knew her, that what he wrote about her is true, or almost so.

We went to what used to be her café thirty or so years ago. That alley spoke to me. It was as if I had been there before.

I need to find her. I wonder where you are and whether you're thinking of going somewhere, like I am.

I closed my journal and freed my thoughts. Maybe they could reach him. I stayed there waiting for them to come back and report to me. My memories came instead. They were about William, our unfiltered chats, his laughs and obsessions, our comfort with each other, our silences, our own spaces. I started asking myself questions that had no answers. Or at least I couldn't find them. Then, exhausted, I walked back home. I didn't feel like doing anything, or perhaps had nothing to do, but it was hard to admit it to myself. So I turned on the TV to a silly show. I was missing something or more than that. I thought I should find out what that was, but fell asleep.

Mario said he would take me out to dinner that night to celebrate the beginning of my summer, and so he did. We went to a restaurant nearby and took a table in its garden that seemed suspended on soft, dim candlelight. Mario ordered two glasses of merlot, *pici*, and a *fiorentina* to share, and as we were seated, waiting for our meal, I heard myself saying once again that I wanted to go look for Clara.

We didn't know her last name and that search would have looked hopeless to everyone. Everyone except me. I didn't know why I wanted to find her. Perhaps I just needed to solve a puzzle. Hers or mine. But again he didn't ask about it, and I too stopped doing so.

We talked about how to organize the search, what to do, and in which order. I told Mario I wanted to visit the places he had mentioned in the story, try to track Clara's friends down, perhaps start with Verde. Verde meant "green" and it was a pretty unusual name for a woman in Italy. Maybe it would be easier to start with her. Verde should know where to find Clara, or at least help us find her. And I wanted to see Perugia. The Umbria Jazz Festival was about to start, and Clara liked that too. And then maybe we could stop in Amalfi and visit the Amalfi Coast. Clara seemed to love that area as well. Maybe she eventually moved there.

Once I sketched our journey, I felt excited. Mario seemed too.

"Will you come with me?" I asked, but at that point I knew what his answer was going to be.

"Is that a question?"

I was right.

After dinner, he told me he wanted to show me something special.

"We have to take a bus, though."

"Can we take a taxi instead?" I asked. I was not a fan of buses.

"It would be better if we took the bus there."

I smiled and agreed on taking the bus. I trusted Mario. Of course I did.

We walked to *Viale Tozzi*, and waited. When the bus arrived, there were only a few passengers. Three guys in their twenties, an elderly lady carrying bags filled with groceries, and two middle-aged women who sat together. Mario and I sat in the back. He said he liked to sit far from people and imagine he was making that journey alone.

"Do you take this bus often?"

"Yes, I think so."

"Isn't it wonderful?" he asked, opening his eyes as wide as he could, trying to see through the night. I looked through the window too. It was mostly darkness, but some of the upper windows of the bus were open, and I could almost taste the green of the countryside amplified by the night dew. I saw houses on the side of the road, some of them with lights on. But they were so few, and seemed to vanish as the bus moved.

Mario placed his left arm around my shoulder and without realizing it, I fell asleep, resting my head on his shoulder. When we arrived, he kissed my forehead and I woke up.

"Monteriggioni," said the driver, sounding sleepy or bored. I had never heard that name before and asked Mario if we were in Siena or Firenze.

"We are in the province of Siena," he said. "Monteriggioni is a town within the province."

The darkness of the night and the evening's wine made me feel suspended, as if I were sleepwalking in a Middle Ages dream. Monteriggioni was, in fact, a medieval town protected by high walls and fortified towers. Mario told me that Dante had drawn inspiration for his *Inferno* from Monteriggioni. That made sense. The town seemed to be enveloped in fog and mystery, and it was more like a village with a plaza, a church, a few houses, an alley of craft and wine shops, and a few small restaurants. Mario waited for my eyes to tour the surroundings, and when they were done, he took my hand and asked me to follow him.

"Here is what I wanted to show you," he then said. "The *Chiesa di Santa Maria Assunta.*" His eyes lay on that church, and he seemed happy, at peace.

"It's often open at night and so sometimes, before going to bed, I come here to pray or watch people making their prayers and lighting candles for them. I don't stay long. Just long enough to feel lighter and ready for sleep. It usually works."

The church was hauntingly beautiful. It seemed Roman or gothic or both. It was plain and evocative, with a travertine façade and what appeared to be brushes of gold. And then, in front of the church, almost a part of it separated by mistake or by a secret design, in the middle of the square, there was a little well made of bricks. Two men were arguing or praying. That peace could have smoothed down anything, and it was hard to see things clearly.

"Shall we go inside?" Mario whispered, as I must have been still dreaming, and he didn't want to wake me up.

I nodded and we walked to the entrance.

The interior of the church was as I had imagined it from the outside. There were a few pews leading to a small altar at the top of three steps. A crucifix to protect the church by reminding its faithful that life was pain. And fresh daisies at the foot of the altar, to remind people that life was beauty too.

And then there was a painting of the Madonna to the left, and the statute of a saint to the right. The Madonna and the saint beckoned from an ancient time and made the entire space feel even more mystic and intimate. That peace slowly seeped into my soul. So I sat on a bench and closed my eyes. When I opened them, Mario was close to me.

"Do you pray?"

"Of course, I do. Who doesn't?" he asked, searching through my eyes.

"I don't always come here to pray, though," he added. "Sometimes I come looking for something. Or maybe my searches are prayers too. Who knows?"

"When you're looking, do you always know what you're looking for?"

"I didn't know before, but now I do. I think I was looking for you," he said, his eyes hugging me.

"I was looking for you too." My words sounded louder than everything I had said in a long time, filling any empty space that was left between us. Yes, we were getting closer and that felt good. He took my hand in his and squeezed it. I felt I could ask more.

"I saw you leaving and coming back home very late at night, and I wondered where you were going at that time. Were you coming here?"

"Most likely." He looked at the altar.

"I find something here," he said. "And sometimes I don't even need to enter the church to feel better. I can stand outside, leaning against the well, waiting for the bricks of the church to mercy me some incense, some peace."

We stayed there for a while, watching people coming and going. Almost everyone left after a while. And when they did, they seemed lighter, as if they had left their burden inside.

A homeless man, though, didn't leave. I wasn't a faithful, and had never been religious, but I prayed for him and myself. We probably had more than my unauthorized prayer in common. When I felt lighter, or both Mario and I did, we left. The homeless man remained. My prayer had worked for me only.

The square now seemed quieter than when we had arrived. Even the two men we'd seen before had left. We crossed the square to the well and leaned against it.

"Isn't it beautiful?" Mario asked, and made the shape of a photograph in front of my eyes as if he were ready to take that photo with his fingers, my eyes pointing to the church's façade against a deep, dark blue sky.

"We have our photo. Now you'll have to write the story."

I heard my silence laughing at me, but thought I could do that. I wanted to.

15

We arrived back in Siena at around one a.m. I should have been tired, but, in fact, the visit to Monteriggioni had energized me. And probably because of that or because of the coffee I drank that day and the several days before that one, I was too keyed up to sleep.

I made more coffee and opened the windows wide to let the night enter. It felt romantic, and I wondered if the night was still holding some treasures for me to discover. No, I couldn't sleep.

I looked for my mac and started my research on Google. I searched for "*Verde e Siena*," "*Verde e Clara*," "*Verde e recitazione*," and used many other keywords, but nothing promising came up.

I took Mario's file and read the story again. Verde was an actress, she was a close friend to Clara, but where was she now? She had fallen in love with someone she met at the Umbria Jazz Festival, but did she live in Perugia? Near there? I searched for hours, going back and forth to the story, looking for clues and details. By the end of the night, I knew that story by heart, and could recite it as a poem, word by word, exactly as Mario had written it. But I had found nothing.

I went to my balcony to breathe in some fresh air, and sat there thinking about the story and the photograph. Mario said Clara had introduced Verde to him as someone who would become a movie star. But what if she never became one? If she had, Mario might have heard of her.

As I was thinking and searching through my thoughts, a poster across the alley captured my attention. Yellow, red, and green waves were wrapping three smiling and welcoming faces, and below them, in big, white letters, the poster read, "*Compagnia della Luna al Teatro del Popolo. Rapolano Terme.*"

Verde was an actress. But what if she was a stage actress?

I went back to my computer and renewed my search. "*Verde in teatro,*" "*Verde a teatro*"... "*compagnia teatrale e Verde,*" "*compagnia teatrale Verde*"...I found it! Or something. A "*Compagnia Teatrale Verde*" was performing *Amicizia* at the *Teatro Sistina* in Roma. Their last performance would be the next day. Verde might well be an actress in that group.

I clicked on the link to the performance and looked for Verde's name among the actors, but it wasn't there. There were three characters in the play and the only female part was played by a woman named Camilla, who appeared to be in her forties. But a theatre company may have more than three actors, I thought, so I continued my search and looked for a list of other performances by the same *compagnia*. The *Compania Teatrale Verde* had performed in many of the most prestigious theatres in Italy, including the *San Carlo* in Napoli, and the *Manzoni* and the *Arcimboldi* in Milano. The reviews of their most recent performances were strong.

I found the troupe's home page and read each actor's bio.

They were a diverse group of men and women, ranging in ages from sixteen on up. Camilla, Maria, Francesca, Arietta, Chiara, Bruno, Davide, Marco, Alessandro, and Gianluca. Unfortunately, there was no Verde.

Finally, I clicked on "*La nostra storia*," and there she was. Verde Svevo, the founder of the *Compagnia Teatrale Verde*. The "story" explained that Verde had created the group about ten years earlier to reinterpret plays that had been written by Italian playwrights in the post-war era. Verde Svevo was sixty-three years old and lived in Roma. She had dedicated her entire life to the theatre and was grateful to her friend, Clara, for having inspired her and her work. "*Bingo*!" as my Milanese colleagues would have said. I got it! I found Verde, and Clara's story began to breathe.

I wanted to run to Mario's apartment, tell him what I had found, but I checked and his apartment was dark. He was likely sleeping.

I bought two train tickets to Roma, two tickets for the *Amicizia*, the play that the *compagnia* was going to stage at the *Sistina* the next day, and I went to bed.

The alarm woke me up at seven. I had slept maybe two hours. I went to my window and saw Mario having coffee while reading his newspaper.

"Mario! We should leave in three hours."

"What? What are you talking about? Leave for where?"

"I found her! You won't believe it!"

"Who did you find?"

"I found Verde. She, I mean, her *compagnia teatrale* will perform tonight at the *Sistina*."

"The *Sistina* is in Roma, Clara."

"Oh, yes, I know. I bought two train tickets and reserved two hotel rooms for tonight."

"*Sei pazza, ragazza*! What if you are mistaken? Do you have a picture of her? How can you be sure she's our Verde?"

Yes, I was sure. Verde, the founder of the company, had dedicated her art to her friend "Clara." What were the odds to find an actress in Italy whose name was "Verde" and whose dear friend was "Clara?" She was certainly our Verde.

"I'm positive. And, yes, I do have a picture of her and I'll show it to you. But you'd better start packing. We have to be at the train station in three hours."

"How many days will we be in Roma?" he asked.

"I have no idea. I bought one-way tickets. If we don't find anything, or even if we're successful, we might go to Perugia or Amalfi from there," I said, a bit worried at how he might react. I really had no plan. Would he be fine with that? But he simply raised his grey eyebrows, laughed, and said,

"*Veramente pazza*."

I found my backpack and stuffed in two pairs of jeans, two shorts, four t-shirts, some underwear, and a sweater. Three hours later, we were on a train to Firenze and, once there, we would connect with a train to Roma.

I had never taken a train in Italy before, and I thought that was quite an experience. Mario had brought a book on movies and, after a while, his face disappeared behind it. But I thought that train and the people traveling on it were too interesting to read or watch anything else.

A family was sitting close to us and, as the train left the station, the older woman, that the children called "*nonna*," pulled from her wide purse giant panini with frittata and broccoli. The frittata's intense aroma quickly filled the entire car, but nobody seemed to notice or care. As I was watching the kids enjoying their meal, the *nonna* turned to me and asked if I would like to join them.

"No, no...grazie," I said, a little embarrassed. Mario stuck his eyes out of the book and smiled.

"You'll love the South."

I thought I would.

And then I looked outside our window. The train was a little noisy, but that noise was almost hypnotic. I fell asleep and I dreamt of Joe. We were going to Roma together and he was holding my hand. In my dream, I loved him and told him. I seemed so sure about it. But then a loud voice said we were in Roma and woke me up too early. Our train was late.

We took a taxi to the hotel, left our suitcases there, and went for a walk.

We strolled along *Via Sistina* and soon came to *Trinita' dei Monti*, the gorgeous church at the top of the Spanish Steps. The city below looked magnificent. We were in Roma.

Piazza di Spagna, at the foot of the steps, appeared solemn and regal, and the comparison with the simple Monteriggioni piazza we had visited the night before was striking. It was only five p.m., but the piazza was crowded. We went down the steps and found ourselves in front of the *Fontana della Barcaccia.* As I was looking at it trying to understand what it represented, Mario explained that the fountain was a half-submerged boat that Bernini had made in memory of the floods of the late sixteenth century. He described more of the fountain's details and I think I lost him at some point. Not because he wasn't clear, but because I was wondering what else I didn't know about him.

"Aren't you an expert?" I said, looking at him, impressed and proud.

"On no, just interested. And I've been here often. Sometimes Gianni and I took the train and spent the weekend shopping. We were exploring beauty, trying to blend with it, disappear in it. We would sit at cafés and read the art books I brought. I'm not sure he liked art that much. He probably just did his best to be part of my life. I wonder if I did my best to be part of his." He looked sad.

"This is the first time I've been to Roma since Gianni..."

I took his hand and dragged him out of his memories to a street artist near the fountain. The artist was telling silent stories to a small crowd that had gathered around him. His eyes looked sad too if you managed to scratch beneath his makeup. But his silent story was a sweet one, perhaps one to heal the artist more than his audience. I hoped it worked for Mario too.

"This is pretty common here," he said.

"What's common?"

"Street performers. They are everywhere you go, and some of them are quite talented."

"Italians seem to be talented artists."

"Sometimes." He smiled.

Had I or the mime succeeded?

I loved when Mario smiled and hated when he was sad. I could not stand it. I did not know how we had become so close so fast, but we had.

The mime's body and facial expressions were sketching a story with many open doors for your imagination to wander. The sketch was beautiful, my wanderings too, although they drew no story. Just random photos and warm feelings.

And then the mime pulled a young girl from the audience, pulled a flower from his sleeves, offered it to her, and bowed. He waited and waited until the girl finally smiled. He then jumped and hugged her. The audience applauded. Would he be happy now? The girl had smiled at him.

"Isn't it interesting?" Mario asked.

"What?"

"When you travel, you're more willing to stop and observe. And you see things you would hardly notice in your daily routine, things that now look so precious and extraordinary to you. You tell yourself there must be something special about that place you're visiting, something that you absolutely miss at home. But life is extraordinary everywhere. You just have to be able to see that."

He was right.

"It takes courage to live," he added. "It takes courage to take chances, to tolerate differences, to understand them, to abandon assumptions and be ready to be surprised by anything that happens around us."

I didn't know what to say. What was he really thinking? His sentence had just sketched a story for me, another one, but I didn't want to fill that sketch with my story. I wanted to hear his own. Something must have hurt him deeply in the past. Was it just Gianni's death? Their hidden love? Was there more I didn't know? Something else, big or bigger, I was missing? I wished he had shared more, but if he wasn't ready, I would have waited. Our relationship was beautiful and perfect as it was. Even its holes and untold stories were.

"Have you ever tried a *gelato* that makes you feel happy?" He pulled me from my questions. I smiled and shook my head.

"No, I don't think I have."

Whether I had or had not didn't really matter. I loved it when he felt he could show me something I did not know.

"Then we must go to *Giolitti*."

That name sounded familiar. Perhaps it reminded me of the artist, Giotto, or someone or something I had seen in an Italian movie. I couldn't say.

As we walked along *Via Condotti*, I lost myself in the sophisticated stores and women walking close to them with multiple fancy shopping bags in their hands. They seemed to be drawing imaginary circles around themselves, holding the rest of the world at a distance.

And we walked through narrow streets, some of them paved with cobblestone, all filled with people.

I stopped in front of a street named *Leoncino*. I looked at the marble plate with that name for a while, trying to memorize it. I loved that name, but that wasn't the first time I had stopped in front of a street name to try to memorize it.

"You won't remember all these names tomorrow, Clara. I'll tell you what to remember when I think you might want to."

We both laughed.

He was right. I forgot almost all the plates and their names. But he was wrong about *Via del Leoncino*, as I never forgot that one. I thought it could be the title of the fairy tale book I might want to write one day. I still do.

Giolitti was an elegant café on *Via degli Uffici del Vicario*, somehow hidden among the many alleys, stores, and *piazzas*. Once there, I followed Mario to an impressive display of *gelati*. I had never imagined there could be that many flavors. I must have stared at that display for quite some time while he waited patiently. The woman waiting to serve us, though, wasn't as patient. Mario noticed and nudged me a bit.

"Shall we order, or do you need more time?"

I had actually not thought about what to get, or perhaps I had, but it was too hard to pick.

"How many can I pick?"

"How many you want, Clara. This is on me."

I chose *stracciatella*, *caffé*, and *cioccolato*. I loved chocolate ice-cream and the idea of trying it in Italy made me excited. Mario ordered *tiramisù* and peach. The woman gave us our *gelati* and we sat at a small table perched on the cobblestones outside the café. Our table was unbalanced but, after a bit, I stopped noticing it. In New Haven, that would have made me uncomfortable. But in Italy everything seemed just perfect, even the imperfections. Mario's idea on discovering beauty while traveling was right.

As we were sinking in our ice creams, I started feeling happy. So Mario was right about that too. An ice cream to make you happy. That is what it was.

"I'd love to learn how to make *gelato*," I then said, my thoughts escaping my mind. "And, maybe, one day, I'd like to buy an ice-cream truck and go around and sell *gelato*. It should be fun and profitable too." He laughed.

"You are quite a character. A lawyer selling *gelati* from a truck? And tell me, where would that be? Los Angeles? New Haven? Siena? Maybe in all of these places?"

Was his a serious question? I carefully pondered it anyhow.

"New Haven, maybe, as it might do some good there. It would bring people a real summer."

We remained silent for a while, perhaps thinking about the ice cream and the truck. At least I was. But then he changed topic.

"Have you thought about what you will tell Verde when you meet her tonight?"

"Do you think she'll be there?"

"Of course she'll be there," he said.

I had not really thought about what I would say or ask, or even how I would introduce myself.

"What if we improvise?" I suggested.

He smiled.

16

Choosing what to wear to the play was easy. I had brought nothing but jeans and t-shirts. I had assumed that the evening would be casual. After all, the play was a comedy. But the theatre was anything but casual. It was overwhelming. Everything was. Red. The rich curtains, the velvet bunting on the stage, the chairs, the walls, the lights. I was wrapped in red. I had never been at a theatre that majestic. Did Clara ever come here? Did she watch her friend perform here? Could she be here tonight? I looked around.

"Who are you looking for?" Mario asked.

Right. Who was I really looking for?

"Isn't that Verde?" He pointed to a beautiful, elegant woman, with long, brown hair. She was wearing a floor-length white dress, gold heels, and had a stunning emerald ring on her right middle finger you could hardly miss. She was talking to an older man wearing a tuxedo, moving side to side while following her, his hands in his pockets, showing authority and knowledge of the topic of their discussion, whatever that was.

"Go talk to her," Mario urged me.

"No, I can't do that now. I will after the show."

"What if she disappears after the show? Come, I'll go with you."

He stood up and started walking toward her. I had no choice.

"*Signora Svevo*?" Mario asked her. "*Sono Mario Pellegrini. Non credo lei si possa ricordare.*"

She looked interested but didn't seem to remember.

"*Sono passati tanti anni. Ero un caro amico della sua amica Clara.*"

As soon as she heard that name, her eyes filled with tears, and she pulled Mario closer to hug him. Then she stepped back, looked at me, and dropped her purse.

"Clara?"

She looked at Mario and then came closer to examine me. She squeezed my arms and stared at me in disbelief. Then she turned to Mario again, waiting for him to explain. As Mario told her about me, Clara's photo, and our search, she kept staring at me, clearly confused by my resemblance with Clara. Then Mario stopped talking and she spoke.

"I haven't seen Clara in over thirty years." She looked sad. "We were close, but our marriages led us down different paths. It was my fault. I fell in love and disappeared. When I realized what I had done, it was too late. Clara had disappeared too. I believe she fell in love with a man she met in Perugia, at the jazz festival. At least, that's what Marta told me. You know Marta, right?"

Mario nodded.

"Yes, I remember her."

"I think Clara married that man," she continued. "I wrote to her several times at her parents' address in Firenze, but never heard back. At some point, I stopped writing."

The play was about to start and a loud voice at a speaker called the audience to their seats. Verde gave us her business card, wrote "*Taverna Trilussa, 24:00*" on it, and said she hoped to see us there, later that night. She then excused herself and quickly disappeared to go backstage.

I put the card in my pocket, and Mario and I returned to our seats. The lights dimmed and the curtain rose.

The *Amicizia* somehow reminded me of *Filumena Marturano*, the play Mario had described in "*Delia's Secret Life*." My instinct was right. Mario later explained that Edoardo De Filippo, the author of *Filumena Marturano*, had also authored the *Amicizia*. He said De Filippo was famous. I had never heard of him, but I liked his stories.

Amicizia was the story of a certain Alberto who had not seen his dying friend, Bartolomeo, for many years, and then finally got an opportunity to spend some time with him before Bartolomeo died. Bartolomeo had a sister, Carolina, who took care of him and tried her best to grant all his wishes. However, Bartolomeo was demanding and hard to please. One day, without even realizing it, Bartolomeo confessed to Alberto that Alberto's eldest son was, in fact, Bartolomeo's son.

I liked that play a lot. I thought it was real, truthful to life, its complexities, ironies, disillusionments, and the many plausible readings of it you could give.

When we left the theatre it was a little after ten p.m. We had two hours before meeting with Verde and her friends, and Mario suggested we walk to *Piazza Trilussa*. He said it would take some time, but we could stop at the *Fontana di Trevi* and the *Pantheon* on our way. I nodded and followed him.

The night was warm and timeless. People and places around me seemed out of focus, and it was for Mario to put them into focus for me from time to time, calling my attention to this or that detail that he thought I should see.

Roma was a theatre, and at some point I felt we had never left *Teatro Sistina*. It was as if we were still watching a play, someone else's or ours, and I wondered about our audience. Would it have mercy on us if we made mistakes?

Fontana di Trevi was spectacular. Mario explained that it portrayed Neptune, flanked by two Tritons, one trying to master an unruly sea horse and the other leading a quieter beast. The two contrasting moods of the sea. There were so many people around the fountain and everyone seemed to be tossing a coin in the water.

"Do you have a coin?" Mario asked.

"Yes, I do."

"Then turn your back to the fountain, make a wish, and toss it in."

"Can I look as I toss?"

"No. You mustn't." He looked at me as if he were describing a holy procedure that could not be altered.

"It will not work unless your back is to the fountain."

Normally, I would have laughed. But I would believe anything Mario said. And so I believed that one too. I followed the procedure. Apparently everyone else there did. Each would turn his or her back to the fountain and then toss the coin in. I watched two girls perform the ritual close to the water. They turned, closed their eyes inspired by their wish, and then tossed their coins over their shoulders, almost at the same time. At some point, there were so many coins in the air that it seemed to be raining coins. I will never forget that image. So many wishes floating in the air and sinking beneath the water. What was my wish? What was I really looking for? Joe? William? My music? Clara? All of them? Was it just a wish per person we were all entitled to? I had all these wishes. I turned and tossed my coin. For all of them.

Our wishes made, we walked to the *Pantheon*.

The *Pantheon* was a majestic dome in *Piazza della Rotonda*, in front of the *Fontana del Pantheon*. The dome was open and we entered. There were few people around, and the room was silent. It wasn't bright, but it wasn't dark either. So where did the light come from? Mario pointed to the ceiling and to a large, circular hole in the dome that opened to the sky. He asked me to close my eyes, and then maneuvered me until he thought he had found the perfect spot.

"Here you go. Open your eyes. Clara, please meet Lady Moon."

The moon was indeed there, full and bright, and I could see it clearly through the ceiling's eye. Shivers ran through my arms and my legs.

"I feel I'm looking at the moon through a telescope," I said, without moving, fearing she could disappear any moment.

"I know. You feel so because you wanted to see her, and your mind silenced the noise. And now you can look at her, see her, her beauty. Your heart is your telescope."

Mario was right. The moon looked like it was near, just beyond the *Pantheon*. I could almost touch it. And the moon's beauty, my shivers, the sky, us there, all were so loud. Rachmaninoff was playing again. My fingers moved, and I let my heart go.

I moved as if I were following a music that only I could hear, and then I felt warm. I turned and turned again. A woman asked her boyfriend or husband to hand her a sweater. She said the dome was cold. Was it?

So the *Pantheon*'s light was a lunar light. I wondered

what happened when it rained and asked Mario. He said that would be taken care by a drainage system below the floor. He showed me some of the holes that seemed part of the floor design. The water would pass through those holes and the system would absorb it.

"Romans were genius," I said. He agreed.

We left the *Pantheon* and continued our walk through *Via Corso Vittorio Emuanuele* and *Campo dei Fiori*. Then we crossed *Ponte Sisto* over the *Tevere*, and finally arrived at *Piazza Trilussa*. It was a few minutes after midnight.

Verde and a group of about fifteen people were seated at a long table in front of the *taverna*. Despite its name, the *taverna* really looked like a *trattoria*. In fact, all the tablecloths had white and red squares on them, so it must have been.

"*Trastevere*," Mario said, turning on himself and breathing in the surrounding. "My favorite neighborhood in Roma."

"Why is that?" I asked.

"It's the *bohemian* feel, I guess."

Yes, I could see that. And *Piazza Trilussa* was probably *Trastevere*'s opening line and its main theme. We were still on a stage.

As soon as Verde saw us, she waved and invited us to join the group. There were two seats left at one end of the table and, although it felt odd, I ended up sitting at the head.

"*Verde, perche' non ci presenti i tuoi amici*?" Arietta asked. I remembered Arietta's name and her face from the website.

"Clara and Mario are friends from Siena," Verde said. "We share a dear friend, also named Clara." Verde looked at us and I spoke.

"Yes, we're looking for Clara. Mario and Verde knew her

well. But I only know her through a photo Mario took of her, and a story he wrote about her. She looks very much like me, and I want, I need to find her." I looked down to avoid seeing my audience's questions. Although I sensed them. What was the meaning of that search, really? This is what they were asking. I knew it was.

"*Pensi che questa Clara sia tua madre o tua sorella*?" one of the actors in the back asked. I laughed.

"*No, no. Mia madre é in Connecticut e non ho sorelle. Almeno, non penso.*"

After dinner, Mario and I waited for Verde to say goodbye to her friends and then the three of us sat on a bench in *Piazza Trilussa* and talked about Clara. Verde thought the story Marta had told her was accurate.

"I remember talking to Marta shortly after Clara's wedding. Maybe Marta had been invited to it, but I'm sure she didn't go. I guess she couldn't. The wedding might have been somewhere in Siena or Firenze, I'm not sure. In any event, I know she didn't go."

"Were *you* invited?" I asked Verde.

"No, I wasn't. By then, Clara and I had lost touch. She was probably upset with me, as she should have been. Or maybe she couldn't find me."

"Have you heard from Marta since then?" Mario asked her.

"Yes. Occasionally. But the last time we spoke about Clara was many years ago."

"Do you know if she still talks to Clara?" I asked.

"I doubt it." Verde's eyes started wandering in empty spaces that were hard to identify. It was dark and it was difficult to read her. "I'm sure she would have told me."

"Do you know where she lives?" Mario asked her.

"Yes, Marta lives in Sorrento. She worked at Clara's

bakery. You probably remember that," she turned to Mario. "Now she has her own. It's also called *Caffé Siena*."

She looked at me to see whether I had more questions for her, and then added,

"We've all been too lazy, too stupid and timid. Everyone makes mistakes, but a true friendship should not just disappear. I am happy you found me and I'd love to help."

I thanked her and asked her for Marta's address. If Mario agreed, I thought it would be nice to go talk to her the next day.

Verde searched her bag, pulled another of her business cards, and wrote, "Marta Frangella. Caffé Siena, Via Fuorimura, 5, Sorrento, Napoli." She then told us that she and her company would be leaving for Napoli the next day. They were scheduled to perform at the *Teatro San Carlo* that week. She explained to me that Napoli was close to Sorrento and if she had a break, she would try to join us in Sorrento, assuming we were still there.

"Clara, Mario, please keep me updated. Tell Marta I miss her, and give her this card for me. She took another of her cards and wrote on it.

Marta mia, mi manchi tanto. Sarò a Napoli nei prossimi giorni e cercherò di venire a trovarti a Sorrento non appena riesco. Verde.

I placed the two cards together with the one she had given us at the theatre, and I thought that, if I had ever had a chance to write the story of Clara, the three cards should be part of it.

"One more thing," I looked at Verde.

"Yes?"

"Can you tell us Clara's last name?"

"It's Bassi. Clara Bassi"

We left, and walked in silence for a while. I thought

about Clara and the actors' eyes I had not checked when I said I wanted to find her. Did they think I was a fool? Was I?

Mario looked at me and seemed to see my questions, or at least, I thought so, as he suggested that we walk some more, perhaps to try to drain or silence them.

"Where would you like to go?" I asked.

"I'm not sure. I'd like to wander a bit with you. Maybe we'll find something else we could hold on to and not let go."

I wasn't sure what he meant by that, but I followed him, my legs almost numb for how much we had already walked. I wondered whether he was as tired as I was. He must have been. But perhaps he thought we or I needed to walk some more, and so we did. We walked and walked, and finally we arrived at a small *piazza* with a fountain raining water on the sidewalk. I wondered if we were still in *Trastevere* but I was too tired to ask him, so I remained silent and just followed him. It was late, perhaps two or three in the morning, but there was a father with his baby girl there. He seemed so happy to see us, almost as if he were waiting for us.

"*Buonasera*," Mario said, and the man smiled, but turned immediately to follow his daughter, who had just started running away from the fountain.

He said she couldn't sleep and so he had decided to take her to the fountain. They lived in one of the buildings around the *piazza*. He pointed to a balcony close to us.

We introduced each other. He was Marco, his baby was Fiammetta.

"She can't sleep," he said, "so I took her here, but she seems afraid of the water."

Yes, I could see that. And I thought I might know why. I was also afraid of the water when I was her age. It took my dad forever to convince me to take those swimming lessons.

He managed to do it only once he showed me that I could swim with my eyes open. I wondered if that was what frightened Fiammetta. Not being able to see under water.

"Maybe she feels she has to close her eyes when going through it, and doesn't like it," I said.

I took Fiammetta's hand and walked her close to the fountain. Then I entered, and let her stay outside the rain, watching me.

"*Guarda che bello, Fiammetta,*" I said, my eyes open.

She looked but then turned away. I didn't move. I stayed there under the water, and started jumping and dancing, pushing the water all around, higher and higher. I laughed, and ran, and laughed some more.

"*Vieni Fiammetta! Guarda che bello!*"

Her father whispered in her ear, asking her to follow me under the water, and she eventually moved, her tiny, chubby foot did. And then she followed.

She walked under the water, her eyes locked on mine, perhaps their safety anchor. And my eyes pulled her, and pulled her, until she was with me, under the water. She started laughing, and ran away. But then came back, and stayed longer, and longer, until it was hard to take her away from it.

We were under the water, running and laughing, and splashing water to each other. Yes, I was happy. And I had found something to hold on to and not let go. I looked at Mario and thought he had too.

17

When we were back at the hotel, I looked for "Clara Bassi" on Google, but for Google she did not exist. I wanted to believe that Google was wrong, and eventually convinced myself that it was. Then I turned off the computer, took a bath, put on a clean t-shirt, and went to bed.

As I lay on my bed waiting for sleep, I kept thinking about the question that actor had asked at dinner:

"*Pensi che sia tua madre o tua sorella*?"

Could Clara be my mother? I'd never thought about that before. That was absurd though, and I couldn't even begin to make sense of it. I closed my eyes, pushed my head against the pillow, and drifted asleep.

When I woke up early the next morning, I ordered a coffee and a croissant filled with apricot jam. My thoughts jumped in the jam and they became sweet. I wrote another letter to Joe.

Dear Joe,

Mario and I are travelling through Italy, looking for Clara, and I love it.

Where are you? Are you playing?

I'm in Rome, sinking in night walks, fountain rains, and apricot jam. I'm collecting stories in a jar for you, stories that press to become songs I might write one day.

At times I miss you, at times I don't, almost happy to be alone, looking for the answers I didn't have for you, for myself, when we met. Will you forgive me and wait for me? If you were here, you and your music would make me forget everything, even that I'm looking. So it's probably good we're not together yet.

I'm learning to look underwater again, as I feel you are there, somewhere, and hope I'll find you or you'll find me. For now, though, I feel I should keep swimming. My eyes have been stuck on the surface for way too long.

I closed my diary and turned on my mac to do some research. I did a Google search for "*Marta Frangella*" and "*Marta e Clara*" but, as expected, I found nothing. I did find a culinary blog that mentioned Marta's bakery in Sorrento with photos of her cakes and original recipes. But that was all.

Getting to Sorrento from Roma would require some effort. We'd need to take a train to Napoli, another from Napoli to Salerno and, once there, a bus to Sorrento. Amalfi was very close. Perhaps we could stop there first.

We left for Amalfi a few hours later.

The train we took looked older than the one we had taken to Roma the day before. The couches still smelled like cigarettes, although Mario explained to me that Italy had had a smoking ban in public places for several years now. The past must have stuck into those couches and perhaps it would never leave, just become older and older, and eventually confuse people. Like the couches' colors, that had almost entirely faded. I thought they must have been red one time. Or perhaps they were brown. Above the seats were some old photos in black and white, showing what I thought must be some iconic places in Italy. I asked Mario.

"Yes, that was Napoli in the early 50s," he said, pointing at one of those photos. "And this one was Roma at the same time."

I looked more closely at the photo of Napoli and started wondering how life could be at that time, whether anyone like Mario and I had made a journey like the one we were making. Did it make sense at that time? Did it now?

We soon arrived in Salerno, and after a short bus trip, we were in Amalfi. We checked into a hotel, left our suitcase, and began exploring the area.

Amalfi was a Mediterranean gem. We walked on the *Lungomare dei Cavalieri*, with the sea first on our left, then on our right. The water seemed to be made of a thousand diamonds glistening in the sun. In fact, the sea was the protagonist, the white buildings, the flowers, and the little cafés across from the sea just a frame for it.

"Did you ever swim in the Mediterranean?" Mario asked, noticing I could not take my eyes off the water.

"No," I said, and felt sorry. In fact, that was the first time I had seen the Mediterranean and felt a strong urge to dive in and feel the water on my skin.

"Let's do it."

"Do what?"

"We'll buy swimsuits and go for a swim."

Mario's ideas often surprised me. Between the two of us, he was the most energetic, the most enthusiastic and, certainly, the most daring. True, the trip had been my idea, and I had arranged our travel plans. But my idea merely looked like a sketch he had turned into a full painting.

"I once thought fairy tales were made-up stories," I said.

"What do you mean?"

"Since I met you I feel I'm living in a fairy tale or a movie that is real, and I don't want it to end."

He smiled, took my hand, and said,

"I'm sure you'll make it last. Let's go buy our swimsuits."

We found a little market that sold everything. Newspapers, *pasta*, *gelati*, all sorts of beach equipment, umbrellas, chairs, and swimsuits.

"Do we need towels?" I asked.

"One should be enough," he said.

I asked the cashier if we could use the store's restroom, and we changed there.

The beach was across the street and we were at the edge of the water before I could think. The water was almost as warm as a bath and even more inviting. As soon as I felt it on my feet I took a deep breath and smiled.

"Isn't that something?" he asked, but before replying, I jumped into the water and dragged him along. I could feel the salt of the sea on my lips and in my hair, and I felt refreshed. The water was so transparent that I could see the stones on the sea floor and little fishes swimming around my feet.

After a while Mario returned to the beach and I stayed swimming for a while.

I thought about the baby girl under the fountain raining water in Rome, and I became her, me at her age, or just my ageless self. I went underwater and opened my eyes. What I saw was beautiful, clean, perfect with its imperfections, deep. And I could hear the sound of waves coming from far away, waves whose existence I had missed when looking at the surface. I opened my eyes wider. Where were they coming from? I couldn't see them but sensed them. There. Underwater. They were light, and were playing with the fishes and the sea stones, moving them softly and making a sound of peace and eternity. I abandoned myself to those waves, and let them play with my heart too, as I wanted to become part of them, part of their sound. Maybe at some point I did.

How could I have forgotten that feeling of discovery over the years? The feeling of looking underwater? How could I have forgotten that I could look underwater? Over the years, I had misplaced that feeling, my courage. I had stopped trying to look underwater, or had forgotten that I could. Why did I stop? Perhaps it was just easier to close my eyes and turn away from anything that needed to be explored, calling "silence" my lack of courage, and blaming it on William or Joe or something else.

But now I was looking underwater again, or at least I was trying to, and I stayed under the Mediterranean water with my eyes open for as long as I could.

When I got out of the water, Mario was on the beach, seated on our towel. I lay myself on the half that he had left for me, wrung my hair, and watched the water drip from it.

"You hair is beautiful," he said, as I sat close to him.

"Thank you. I'm planning to cut it though."

"Why?"

I really didn't know how I came up with that idea. Perhaps it was the sun, the sea, the need to be braver again, the need to experiment.

"Changes," I then said, picking one of the options that my heart was suggesting. "Let's find a hairdresser. I need to do it today."

"Just like that?"

"Yes. Just like that."

"Short?"

"Very," I said, and smiled.

We stayed on the beach and relaxed, each on their little

corner of the towel. I felt the warmth of the sun on my body and surrendered to it. Then the salt dried on my skin. I could feel it around my lips, my eyebrows, in my hair. When I was dry, or almost so, we left.

We wandered on the *Lungomare* and eventually found a hairdresser. The name of the shop was "*Amelia*." I looked inside and saw a woman in her forties working on an older woman's hair and laughing with her perhaps for a story the woman had told her. The hairdresser seemed sweet and elegant, and I loved her short hair. It reminded me of a photo of Audrey Hepburn I had seen somewhere. She saw that I was looking inside her salon and called me in.

"*Signorina, vuole tagliare i capelli*?"

"*Sì*," I said.

"*Vienga dentro*."

When I turned to Mario to see whether he approved, he walked in. I guess he had approved.

"*Sedetevi, prego*."

She invited us to sit and wait, occasionally smiling at us as she worked with her customer.

When it was my turn, I explained to her that I wanted the same haircut as hers.

"*Oh, è facilissimo. Mi prenderà on'oretta, non di più*."

"Would you mind waiting?" I asked Mario.

"Not at all. But I'll wait for you at the café we passed, just down the street. I want to be surprised."

I winked at him, and said I would meet him there when I was done.

Amelia washed my hair, then cut it with a studied precision. We didn't talk much. My Italian had significantly improved since I'd arrived in Italy, but I remained silent and let her take care of me. I wanted to think about the things I had seen or failed to see underwater until that very moment. And I wanted to be surprised too. So I remained with my eyes closed for the entire time it took her to complete my surprise. And when she was done, I indeed was. Surprised and happy. And maybe braver too. At least I hoped so.

"*Voilà*!" she said, and handed me a mirror. Was I looking at myself? Was that me?

"*Le piace*?"

"*Mamma mia*!" I replied.

"*Posso prenderlo come un 'sì'*?"

"Oh, yes, definitely...*cioè, sì*!"

I thanked Amelia, assuming that was her name, paid her, and started walking to the café where Mario was waiting for me. Then my Blackberry buzzed, I checked and saw an email from William.

Hey,

How is it going over there? I'm planning my trip to Italy. What about the last week of September? Would that work? The idea of seeing you again makes me happy already. Hope all is well.

William

I was happy to read that email, and immediately replied that, sure, it was fine. I paused and looked around. I was truly in a different world, with a new haircut, with a new friend. I wondered if William might like that. How will it be to speak with him again? As I asked these questions, I went to find Mario. As soon as I turned the corner, I saw him standing in front of the café.

"Clara! *Bellissima*! You are a vision."

"Really?"

"Yes, really. What do you think?"

"I think I love it," I said.

"Had you been planning this? The haircut, I mean? I

remember you telling me that you had worn your hair long most of your life."

"Yes, I had, but had not planned this. I might have decided to do it when I was swimming."

"I had that feeling. A moment of inspiration, right?" He hugged me and said he wanted to show me around. I was ready.

"William is coming to visit me this September," I then said.

"How nice."

"You'll like him a lot. In fact, everyone does."

From the café, we walked to the Amalfi Cathedral, "*il Duomo di Amalfi*," as Mario introduced it to me. The *Duomo* differed from those I had seen in Siena and Roma. Various styles, Roman, Arab, and Byzantine blended in it to create its unique beauty. And yet the stairs to the *Duomo* reminded me of the Spanish Steps and *Trinita' dei Monti*, as with *Trinita' dei Monti*, the stairs made the *Duomo* appear even more unreachable, otherworldly.

"I would love to get married here one day," I said.

"I would love that too."

"Would you be my witness?"

"Of course. I'll always be."

We climbed the stairs, entered the *Duomo*, and looked inside. The interior was majestic. There was gold everywhere and the ceiling seemed to reach beyond the sky. I felt I could still hear the waves and their sound. Had the Mediterranean ever entered the *Duomo*? Had it stuck into my hair? Was it the haircut? I smiled and closed my eyes to keep that sound with me, and I wondered if Mario could hear that too, if anyone else could.

When we stepped outside, Mario asked if we should meet with Marta. I checked the time.

"Her bakery might be closed by now." It was five. To get to Sorrento, we would need to take a bus. The chances of her bakery being open by the time we arrived there were slim.

"You could call and see."

Mario was right, and I did as he suggested.

I found the bakery's number on my Blackberry and dialed it. A woman answered. It was Marta. I explained who I was and she told me she had already spoken with Verde that morning. She did not seem excited to meet with us, but agreed to do so. She said the bakery would remain open until at least seven p.m., and that the bus should get us there by then. I said we would be there by that time, and she promised to wait for us.

And so we took the bus to Sorrento.

That bus was tall and intimidating. I had never taken a bus like that before and I was scared considering the roads ahead.

"This must be new to you," Mario said, noticing my firm grip on the seat's arm. "Let's sit in the front where we can watch the road."

I nodded without confirming that he was right. I didn't want him to think that I was scared when, in fact, there was no reason to be. If he felt comfortable taking that bus, I should as well. But I didn't. And seating in the front didn't help. So when the bus pulled away from the square, I unconsciously grabbed the arm of my seat again. Mario smiled and placed his hand on mine. I thought about saying that everything was fine, that there was no need. But I thanked him with my eyes, as I realized that I in fact needed that, especially when the bus started taking sharp bends on a road that overlooked the sea.

I could actually see the sea below, it looked so close that

we seemed to be flying just above it. I felt the bus could careen off the street any moment, but the driver seemed not to care or was just too casual about it.

I looked for my hair and touched it. I had promised, hadn't I, to be braver. We arrived in Sorrento just before seven and I did survive.

The bakery was on *Via Fuorimura*, a short walk from our stop. It was still light and not as hot as it had been in Amalfi. We saw people on bicycles, others riding *vespas*, and others sitting and chatting on the chairs and benches that lined the street. At some point, the street became a narrow canyon of houses, some villas with lovely courtyards, some more modest ones. The scent of jasmine was everywhere.

We saw *Caffé Siena* as soon as we turned on *Via Fuorimura*. The bakery was small, with a white canopy protecting that little shop from the rest of the world. We entered and saw a woman in her late fifties talking to a young girl who called her "*nonna*."

"Marta?"

I called her name and she immediately turned toward me.

"*Ciao, sono Clara.*"

"*Ma tu sei...la figlia di Clara*?"

"*No, no. Questo è Mario.*" I let Mario come forward and she immediately recognized him.

"*Sì, sì, certo, mi ricordo di Mario. Come state?*" she asked, looking at us and then turning to check on her granddaughter.

"*Questa è Lucia, mia nipote. Ha tre anni.*"

The baby was adorable. A doll in a flowered dress, socks with little laces, and a pair of black shoes with two little holes on top.

"*Ciao Lucia*," I waved at her, but she hid behind her grandmother's dress, peeking out of it from time to time.

Marta invited us to sit at a table on a corner of her bakery and offered us coffee and pastries. Her café reminded me of Clara's. And it wasn't just the name. The walls were painted a soft yellow and there were plants with little blue, red, and violet flowers resting on shelves built into the walls. The *pietra lavica* floor in a light shade of green felt like a refreshing match to the flowers and the walls. And the display case was modest, but the variety of pastries impressive. Just like in Clara's café.

When Marta returned with our coffee and pastries, she smiled and joined us at the table. She was not hostile as I had feared from our chat on the phone. Just simple, straightforward, genuine. She told me that I reminded her of Clara and that, had it not been for my strong foreign accent and my short hair, she would be sure to be talking to her, as if time had stood still. I told her that was why I was searching for her.

She listened carefully to our story and then told us a bit about Clara and the last time she had spoken with her. It might have been thirty years ago now. At that time, Marta was in Roma visiting her grandparents. Clara was in Siena and told Marta that she was about to marry someone, but they hadn't decided where they would live. "Not in Siena," Marta recalled Clara saying. Clara promised to send Marta her new address and told her that she was expecting a baby and would bring it to Siena once he or she was born. But that was the last time the two talked. Marta wrote to Clara at her parents' address in Firenze but, at some point, perhaps five years later, her letters started coming back as being sent to the wrong address.

Then Marta married and moved to Sorrento as her

husband was from there. She opened her own bakery, had three children and Clara slowly vanished between Marta's family and her business.

What if Clara couldn't respond to Marta's letters? Had Marta thought about it? What if she had become ill? What if she died? When those questions stole my breath, Mario noticed and tried to pull me away from them.

"Marta, would you like to see Clara again?"

Marta looked down and said she would have preferred if Clara had looked for her. But then, confessed that, yes, she would like to see her again.

I asked Marta if she still had the address of Clara's parents and if she would mind if we called with any other questions we might have. She nodded and retrieved the address from a worn address book she kept in a drawer beneath the cash register.

I thought I somehow had managed to connect with her. I hugged her and handed her the card Verde had asked us to give her. I put the address in my pocket, and we left. The last bus to Amalfi was just about to leave.

On the bus, I placed my head on Mario's shoulder and thought about the day. And perhaps because it was dark and I could see very little, or perhaps because I had been on that bus and on that road earlier that day, I felt I could trust it this time and was no longer afraid. I relaxed and looked at the coast, speckled with lights that looked like fireflies in the night. I thought about the people I had met, my discoveries, and confessed to myself that the Clara I was looking for was the one seated on the bus. And that confession made me feel better.

Even if I never met Clara Bassi, I was looking for Clara Smith, the one underwater.

In my heart, though, I hoped to find both.

18

Our *albergo* in Amalfi was simple, but with a wonderful view of the beach. That night, I left the window open and fell asleep to the sound of the waves breaking on the rocks, and returning to do the same again, and again.

I dreamt about Clara. She was walking on the sea's edge, barefoot. Her hair was long, as in the photo, slightly covering her face. She was moving slowly along the seashore, and she seemed to be looking for something she had lost. In the water. I called her name. I wanted to help her find whatever that thing was. She did not turn.

"I can swim with my eyes open. My father taught me that, I can show you."

"I know you can," she replied, and I could feel her smile. But I still couldn't see her face and I begged her to turn toward me.

"Not yet," she whispered.

I woke up and went to the window to check whether that was a dream. It had seemed so real. The night was dark and the edge of the sea was deserted. I returned to my bed and slowly, perhaps at dawn, finally fell asleep.

The next day Mario and I had breakfast at a café close to our hotel. We talked about our plans. I told him I wanted to go to the Umbria Jazz Festival in Perugia. He liked the idea, but suggested that we spend another day in Amalfi, perhaps visit Positano, and then leave the next day for Perugia.

"Sounds like a plan," I said, and winked at him.

He sat back and turned to the thriller he had bought at *Roma Termini*, while we were waiting for the train for Napoli. I had my computer with me and did some research on Perugia and the jazz festival. I found the program. It was dense with details. The festival began on July 6 and ran through the 15th. Ten days of jazz, starting each day at noon and continuing until midnight and beyond. I checked the schedule for the next day and my eyes locked on the name, "Joe Gray." Joe was going to perform at the Umbria Jazz Festival? The next day? That could not be true.

I took my eyes off the screen to set them and myself straight, and then checked again.

Yes, that was actually happening. Joe was going to play in Perugia the next day.

I looked for a pen to write down the information and spilled my coffee all over our table and on my computer. I must have turned purple when Mario asked me if anything was wrong.

"You will never believe what I just found," I said.

"I'll try." He smiled and placed his book on the side.

"Joe is performing with his band tomorrow night at eight, at the *Giardini Carducci* in Perugia."

"Are you serious?"

My heart was beating so fast it was almost impossible to say another word. And so he continued,

"We should go."

"Yeah, sure."

"No, I mean it. We should go."

"I don't know. What if I see him?"

"You should see him and talk to him. In fact, you should send him an email and tell him that you are in Amalfi and you'll be there tomorrow."

"I wouldn't know what to write. How would I explain...?"

"Maybe you're just trying too hard."

I thought about his words, but still felt I needed more time. I did not want to do anything in a rush. I'd already done that and it didn't work. I needed time to think, or maybe, time not to think, and just let the possibilities evolve. In any event, whatever I would do, it wouldn't be an email. I asked Mario to put that topic on hold, and promised we'd resume it at the end of the day. He didn't seem happy about it, but finally agreed to let me handle it my way. He trusted me. I knew he did.

I placed Joe in the back of my mind and checked the bus schedule. A bus for Positano would be leaving in ten minutes from our *piazza*. I turned and saw a big *SITA* blue bus, parked right there. The driver was checking tickets and welcoming passengers aboard. The bus had a little white sign on it with the names of the stops it would make on its route. Positano was on that list, and on ours too. We paid the fare and got on the bus.

Positano reminded me of Amalfi and Sorrento. Square, pastel colored houses clung to the steep slopes of mountains overlooking the sea. The mix of opulent villas and modest homes was framed with gardens and *bougainvillea*, the more modern houses on the lower part of the mountain, and the older, more dramatic ones above. Mario insisted that we rent a *vespa*. It was white and it seemed safe, although the owner insisted that we wear helmets, "*sempre.*"

Our day in Positano went by quickly. We drove on streets and alleys that were wide and narrow, sometimes wider or narrower than we expected. We stopped at shops that had all sorts of items on display, and had lemon *granita* on a bench in front of a sunset that was pure poetry. And then we stopped for a while near the beach, somehow lost in the beauty of the *Chiesa di Santa Maria dell'Assunta*, a gorgeous church whose cupola was covered with yellow, blue, and green majolica tiles.

We saw so many things, but I don't remember their details. I remember the colors, the smells, our laughs, and I remember our silences. I was thinking about Joe and wondering if we would meet the next day and what we would say to each other if we did. Mario's silences seemed filled with peace. He was enjoying the surroundings, while perhaps revisiting his memories. He told me that he and Gianni loved the Amalfi Coast and that they had spent much time there.

We went to bed early that night and I was happy to feel too tired to think or ask myself questions that had no answers.

The next day the loud voice of a man calling to a "Francesca" woke me up. Mario and I had not talked about Perugia and Joe the night before as I had promised, but when I opened my eyes, I felt ready to go.

I reserved two rooms at an elegant hotel in front of the *Giardini*, where Joe was scheduled to play that night. Most of the hotels in Perugia were fully booked because of the festival. The location of our hotel was perfect, and although the price was a bit over the top, somehow I thought we deserved a treat, and I wanted our night there to be special.

The hotel was indeed beautiful. It had an expansive terrace overlooking the city, and an elegant hall and restaurant. The rooms were spacious, and had been decorated in a regal, nineteenth century style.

Once in my room, I placed my shorts, shirts, and jeans on the bed and realized I had nothing appropriate for the night, so I went out for some quick shopping.

It was hot, and the sunlight was so strong that everything appeared as beneath a bright patina. The streets were crowded with tourists, locals, and people of all ages. Everyone was upbeat and filled with jazz. It was clear that the entire city was celebrating, and I wanted to celebrate too.

Most of the shops were a little too hip for me, but then I found one more to my taste, and as I was studying the store's window and deciding whether to enter, I heard someone call my name.

"Clara?"

I turned and there he was.

Joe was standing a few feet from me, staring in disbelief. We looked at each other in silence, neither of us knowing what to say. His hair seemed longer and more out of control than the last time I had seen him. He had noticeable, heavy black bags around his eyes, and his usual beard. He seemed to have lost weight.

"I thought you were in Siena."

"I am. I mean...I was. I'm traveling with a friend. Mario. You remember?"

"What?"

No, he couldn't remember, as I had never sent him my letters.

"You're right. I didn't tell you about him, actually. Mario, my friend, is helping me find...." He turned, his look a mix of disappointment and disapproval.

"He's in his eighties," I added, but his look did not change.

There was more silence. He looked down, trying to avoid looking at me, but then he looked up.

"That's nice," he said. "I hope you find whatever you're looking for. You cut your hair?"

"Yes, I did. Do you like it?"

"Yeah. Sure." His voice was toneless and he now seemed to be looking past me.

"How are you? How is Sarah?" I asked.

"She's O.K., I guess. I haven't seen her since, well, since you left."

"How are you, Joe?"

He paused and stared at me.

"I'm fine." Then he bit his lip, perhaps trying to resist the urge to say more, but then surrendered.

"I still don't know what happened between us. I thought it was one thing, you thought it was another. Then you disappeared. No emails, texts, nothing."

My heart was racing. I wanted to ask him to hug me, to hold me.

"I know," I said. "I thought about writing, but every time it seemed so hard. And you didn't write either."

"Well, the most important thing is that you're happy now."

"I'm trying to be."

"That's good," he said, seeming to end our conversation.

"Are you happy?" I asked.

He didn't reply. He gave me the same intense look he had given me the night before I left for Italy. I wanted to say more, I wanted to ask him if we could go somewhere, sit down and chat, like that night in the bar, but I couldn't.

There was an awkward emptiness in the center of the crowded street. I tried to fill it, but no words came.

"Listen," he said, "I have to go. My band is waiting for me to rehearse."

"Joe?"

"Yes."

"I'm just trying to understand why I ran away from you, why I was so scared…"

He turned, walked away before I finished my sentence, and quickly disappeared into the crowd. No, he didn't want to hear my excuses, assuming I had one. I felt crushed.

I walked back to the hotel, my legs heavier and heavier each step I took. When I was in my room, I lay on the floor, on my back, and remained still for a while, staring at the ceiling. I felt pain, and it was strong, but I couldn't say where it came from. It seemed everywhere. It was as if my memories, my fears, my failures, my doubts had all reappeared waiting to confront me. They were showing no mercy. And at some point they became so loud that I had to close my eyes hoping the darkness would silence them. I tried to rest, but I couldn't.

And soon it was time to go to the concert. But I wasn't sure I wanted to go. I pressed my hands against the floor trying to find the courage to decide, and finally stood up, and dragged myself to the bathroom.

I took a shower, changed, and went to the lobby later than what Mario and I had agreed. I saw him talking to an elegant woman in her forties. He was complimenting her on her shoes and she looked flattered.

"*Eccomi*," I said, looking at him.

He stood up, offered me his arm, and we left the hotel.

"I saw him," I then said. "I ran into Joe this afternoon."

"When?"

"I thought I needed something better to wear tonight. I went shopping and, as I was looking around, I bumped into him."

"And? Did you talk?"

"Kind of. But we didn't say much. It was hard. I told him I was trying to understand why I ran away from him."

"And?"

"He walked away before I could even try."

"But do you now know why you ran away from him?"

"Actually, I don't. I'm sure talking to him would have helped though, and I felt bad that we didn't have a chance. He was late for his concert. But I think he didn't want to talk to me."

"Perhaps you can meet tomorrow."

We stayed silent for a while as I was trying to think of a way to talk to Joe that night.

"I have to talk to him tonight." I made up my mind.

"But how? Do you know where he's staying?"

"No."

"Is there any way we can find out?"

"I doubt it."

"We could try to meet him at the concert."

"You say it in a way that seems easy, but it's not. I'm sure it's not," I said, but I hoped I was wrong.

"We'll make it work," Mario said, taking my hand in his.

We arrived at the *Giardini* half-an-hour before the concert and tried to press our way up to the stage. The venue was packed. There were areas where the crowd was less intense, and others where it was just impossible to pass. But we were resolute, edging forward slowly but steadily, and we finally got close to the stage just as Joe was about to climb the stairs.

"Joe!" I yelled at him and he turned.

"What are you doing here?"

"I need to talk to you. Come down."

"I can't. We're on next."

"Can we talk after the concert? Please?"

He resisted, hesitated, then looked at the rest of his band and said,

"O.K. Wait for me at *La Bottega*, in *Piazza Morlacchi*. I'll be there right after midnight."

I wrote the name of that place on my Blackberry, and Mario and I moved to a spot where we could watch the show.

It was terrific. The audience loved their music. I recognized some of their pieces from that night at the Jazz Place, but some seemed new. As I was listening to their music, I remembered us. I thought about the things I might want to say to him later. I tried to explain our last night together to myself so that I could explain it to him, but I failed. I tried and tried, but what I found sounded just like empty excuses. He was there, though, and I was too. So I had to try harder.

Joe and his group finished playing at around eleven. Mario wanted to take me to *La Bottega*, and I would have loved to walk there with him, but it was late, we were both exhausted, and so I told him I would take a taxi to that place, and wait for Joe there. And so I did.

I got to *La Bottega* a little before midnight. There was a bench at the entrance and I sat there and waited. I waited and waited. It seemed endless. At two in the morning, I decided to leave. Joe had not come and I had nodded to sleep on that cold and unfriendly bench two or three times already. I called a taxi and returned to the hotel.

19

As the taxi drove me to the hotel, I crashed into my emptiness. I really needed to talk to someone, but I was sure Mario was asleep. When I got to my room, I looked at the clock and thought I could call my father. It would be almost nine p.m. in New Haven.

"Hi, dad, it's me."

"Clara, hi. How are you? How is it going over there?"

"It's going well. I'm in Perugia."

"Perugia? I thought you were in Siena?"

"I finished the last project I was working on and left for a brief trip with Mario."

"Mario?" He was surprised to hear that too, and I realized I had not shared with him many important details of my life of the past several months. I asked him if he had time to talk and I tried to fill in the holes that I had unintentionally (and sometimes intentionally) left in my weekly reports to him. So I told him about Mario, his photos, and the photo that had dragged us on that journey.

"What's the name of this woman?"

"Clara. Just like me. Can you believe it? Are you there?"

"Yes, yes, I'm here. You say she looks like you?"

"Yes, very much like me."

"Where was the photo taken?"

"In Siena, at her own café, *Caffé' Siena*. Sometime in the sixties."

"Hmmm....And why are you looking for her?"

"That photo set me off balance. And the story Mario wrote for it seemed to be my story. I've been visiting the places that she loved, and I feel a deep attachment to all of them. Roma, Amalfi, Positano, Sorrento, Perugia. And I met and talked to her friends Verde and Marta. I haven't found her yet. But, I found out something. I know that Clara disappeared without explanation more than thirty years ago. I know her last name—"Bassi"—and Marta gave me Clara's parents' address in Firenze. Clara's friends told me that she married a man she met in Perugia, and they lost track of her afterward. They looked for her, but couldn't find her."

I paused and thought about what I had just said. I had been talking rapidly, perhaps too much so for him to be able to absorb everything I said. But I was afraid that if I stopped and waited for him to give me his thoughts, he might say that my search was a crazy idea, and I didn't want to hear that. But then I took my risk, took a deep breath, slowed down, and asked him if he was following.

He said that he was, and I continued.

"I think Clara had a strong effect on Verde and Marta." I told him about them and how I thought she had influenced them. Then I paused, poured a glass of wine, sat back on the big chair close to my bed, and asked him what he thought. He did not answer and instead asked me how I was.

"I'm...fine." I was confused by that question. We had talked about it already, hadn't we?

"You seem anxious or sad, or both. Am I right?"

Yes, he was. Of course he was.

"I'm sad."

"Why?"

"I saw Joe tonight, but didn't really have a chance to talk with him."

I told my father about the last night in Los Angeles and the meeting with Joe in Perugia, my waiting at the restaurant earlier, and his not showing up.

"What would you have told him if you had a chance?"

"That I miss him, that I'm writing him letters almost every day just to feel I'm actually *talking* to him. That I'm trying to understand myself and why I let him go that night. Though I probably still don't know that. Any of it."

"So it's probably better he didn't show up."

"Maybe," I said, and felt the warmth of the wine in my arms and my chest. The pain numbed a bit, or I just started losing my filters. I cried.

"I think we should talk," my father said.

"We are talking."

"Not on the phone. Not like this. I need to come over there and we should talk about what you're going through."

I thought it was odd that my father would take a flight to Italy just to talk to me. But I felt so drained and I needed him close, so I didn't even try to talk him out of his idea. Knowing he would come made me feel better. After we hung up, I rested my head on the pillow and slept.

The next morning I woke up later than usual. Mario must have passed by and slipped an envelope under my door. His note said he would be having coffee in the lobby and wait for me there. I washed my face quickly and, without changing from the night before, went straight to the lobby. When Mario saw me, he smiled.

"Someone did not get back to the hotel last night..."

"Oh, no, I did come back. I just fell asleep without changing. I felt so bad that I couldn't even do that."

He looked at me for a moment, trying to decide if I was joking, but quickly realized that I wasn't.

"Joe didn't show up," I said, looking for an explanation, an idea. "He didn't show up. I waited until two and then called a taxi and came back to the hotel. Why did he do that?"

He took my hand, pulled me to the chair close to him, and made me sit.

"He looked sad when we saw him, when he was about to go on stage. I don't think he meant to hurt you. Actually, I think he's hurt. Perhaps he was afraid too."

"Yes, I thought that. But, not a text, an email...?"

"Have you checked to see whether you got anything from him last night or this morning?"

No, I had not checked. I found my Blackberry in my pocket, turned it on, and looked in my inbox and...yes, there it was.

From: jgray@aol.com:
To: Clara.Smith@bb.com

3 a.m. (7 hours ago)

Clara,

Seeing you yesterday was hard. These months have been hard. I first tried to understand what happened between us, but then gave up. You disappeared. It hurt. I'm sorry for not showing up. I hope you find whatever you are looking for.

Joe.

"I think this man is in love with you," Mario said, "but you should be sure about your feelings before you talk to him again. You don't want to hurt him again."

Mario was right. I missed him though, and yet I felt unresolved, uncertain about who I was and what I wanted. I had to understand that first.

"You're right," I said, and looked at him hoping he would also tell me what to do next.

"I think we should go back to Siena and, maybe, we could do some more research on Clara from there, if you feel like it. If we need to go to Firenze to look for her or her family, it'll be easy to do that from there."

I remained silent and looked down, unsure of what to do.

"I think you should rest now," he added, "and I think it's time to go home."

Yes, it was.

20

We returned to Siena that afternoon and I had a few days for myself, to relax and prepare for my father's arrival. He arrived that weekend.

I told him I could meet him at the airport in Firenze, but he insisted on taking a taxi. My father had always been precise and attentive to details. But he hadn't travelled abroad that much, and it surprised me to see him so well informed on travel from Firenze to Siena.

I was excited for his arrival and waited for him on my balcony. When I saw his taxi pull up and then his big smile, I ran downstairs and hugged him. My hug was so strong he had to fall back to the passenger's seat to catch his balance.

"Clara, you cut your hair. Oh, my."

"Yes, I did. I forgot to mention that." I was afraid to ask him what he thought. I knew he loved my long hair. He did seem a bit disappointed.

"You look so different. Nice. But different."

He looked at me again, took a quick look around, and then we went upstairs. He placed his carry-on bag on the floor, came into the kitchen, and seemed impressed by my *crostata di pesche e amaretti*. We sat at the table, and he asked me how I was and if I had discovered anything more about my Clara.

"I'm better, especially now that you are here. No, nothing new on Clara. To be honest, I've tried to distract myself for the past few days. Not much energy."

"Have you spoken with Joe since that night in Perugia?" he asked.

"No. He sent me an email saying he didn't feel like meeting with me that night, and that he was sorry for not showing up. I haven't replied."

"Why not?"

"I really don't know what to say." And I didn't want to talk about Joe either. So I changed topic. "I'm happy you're here. You need to meet Mario."

"Oh, yes, I'd love to meet him. The man who took the photo that made you travel, right?"

"Yes, a wonderful person. I'm sure you'll like him a lot."

"Can I see the photo?" he asked.

I went to my bedroom and searched my backpack, which I had yet to unpack. The file was in there, stuffed between my jeans and t-shirts. I placed it in front of him on the kitchen table. He took it in his hands. They were visibly shaking. He opened the file and stared at the photo, and then placed it back in the file.

"Is there anything wrong? Dad?"

He didn't respond. He went to the balcony and stared out for a while. I sensed he was feeling uncomfortable, but couldn't say why.

"Is everything O.K. with you and mom?"

"Why don't we go for a walk?" he asked. "Would you like that?"

"Sure."

I grabbed my phone and we left.

"I'd like to walk along the city's walls."

The walls he was referring to surrounded the city and had been built between the tenth and the eighteenth centuries. I had seen portions of them before, but had not walked along them, and I liked that idea a lot. How did he come up with it?

"Did you read a travel guide before coming?" I asked.

"No. Someone took me on this walk before."

"Oh."

"There are a few things about me you don't know," he said. Then he took a deep breath and began his story.

"Before you were born I was a different person. I felt I was leading a charmed life. I had met the woman of my dreams and was madly in love with her. We met in New York, at the Blue Note. I believe it had just opened. She was Italian. Your mother was Italian. Born in New York."

"What?"

Clara?

"Her name was Anna."

"What are you talking about? I don't understand."

"Let me finish. I know it's confusing, but it'll be easier if you just listen."

He took my hands and looked into my eyes, begging them to let him talk.

"You know how much I love you and you know I'd never do anything to hurt you. If I didn't tell you this story before, there was a reason. Please let me finish, and then you'll decide whether I betrayed your trust."

His pain was penetrating. I could almost feel it in my throat. Or was it my pain? It was hard to say. At that point, I was more than confused. I lowered my head and let him to continue.

"I was living in New Haven at the time, completing my Ph.D. in physics. Spent most of my time alone in a lab. But one weekend, a few friends convinced me to spend a weekend in New York. On the second night, we went to the Blue Note. I didn't know much about jazz, but went along for the ride even though I was close to broke.

"And that's where I met Anna. She was friend of a friend of a friend, and I couldn't take my eyes off her. At some point, we found ourselves sitting together and we started chatting. She brought something out in me. I was flirting with her and she flirted right back. Pretty unusual for me Do you remember Maria and Alfredo?"

I nodded.

"They were her parents, your grandparents."

Maria and Alfredo? Of course. They always treated me like family. I remembered the time Maria asked me to call her "*nonna*." My mother told me what that meant, and I thought that was so sweet. I had no idea.

"That night, I couldn't afford a hotel room, but I didn't want to go back to New Haven. I wanted to be with her, and was so happy when she offered to keep me company after the concert. We spent the night walking up and down Manhattan, talking and laughing until the sun came up. I was completely lost in her beauty."

His eyes filled up with tears and since we were approaching a bench, I asked him if he wanted to sit and take a break. But he said he preferred to walk and so we did.

"She taught dance at a studio in Brooklyn. Actually, she danced whenever she moved, whenever she talked. She was an angel sent to this world by mistake." He smiled and seemed to see her, right there. I wished I could have too.

"She was pure and naïve, almost a baby in the body of a woman, unaware of the world around her. I fell in love with her that first night. And, no, I didn't have time to ask her whether she liked to travel, whether she liked Dostoyevsky or comedies, whether she liked theatre or opera, whether she loved her parents, whether she liked Italian cuisine, what was her favorite dish, and whether she could cook. But I was just...I knew she was the one."

His tears became louder. I had never seen my father cry, and that was hard. It cracked my heart, and I decided that, no matter what his story was, I could never be angry with him. I knew he loved me and whatever he had done, he had done out of love.

He took another deep breath, looked at me trying to understand what I was thinking and then asked me if I was O.K. I said that I was, and I hugged him and kissed him on his cheek.

"I'm sorry," I said. And I was. For him. For myself. For her.

"I could not afford losing you, Clara. You are what is left from our love, my most precious thing in this world."

I took his hand in mine. We had completed our first tour of the city along its walls and had just come back to the point where we had begun. But we continued. We walked that trail four times until it was late into the night, until my legs and my feet ached. But he needed to keep moving, he needed to be where he was. We followed that trail without even thinking about what we were doing and, at some point, he seemed to be in a trance, and I was probably in it with him. He was telling a story that he seemed to be reading straight from his heart. And I was listening, trying to picture everything he said and pulling myself into it without questioning the story or his recollection. If I interrupted him with any question or comment, I would have probably awoken him and everything would be lost. So I remained silent, and followed his steps.

"We kissed that night, and there was no part of me that didn't feel it."

I remembered my kiss with Joe, and then somehow thought about William's kiss. They were so different, but I had felt both deeply. Perhaps the same way he had.

"From that night on we were together. I spent many hours in her dance studio working on my dissertation."

The ballet, her passion for jazz, their kiss…it all made sense.

"Her parents were originally from Siena and her dream was to visit there. It was May and I wouldn't start teaching until August. We rented an apartment and spent the summer in Siena. So, yes, I have been here before.

"Our time in Siena was a dream. We visited every corner of the city and the countryside. She'd read a lot about Siena, and seemed to know everything about it, so she was the perfect guide. She loved when I told her that. By that time, she was six months pregnant with you. But she was so energetic and enthusiastic that it was impossible to slow her down. I was happy about our time in Siena, but I was also looking forward to going back to start my new job. And yet I wasn't sure she would like Hartford, and I was worried that taking her from Brooklyn would be harsh on her. She seemed to take her oxygen from her dance studio, her students, her friends."

We quickly stopped at a market and got some water, but then he continued as if there had been no pause.

"She was a wonderful dancer. We had a small apartment here, and at times, she would dance or play jazz for me on the old piano we had rented, and I felt the happiest and luckiest man on earth. That angel who loved me and loved me only, was my woman.

"One day, I left to go for a walk while she was making lunch and I bought an engagement ring. At night, I took her for a walk at the *Giardini La Lizza* and, then, when it became dark and she started feeling cold, before taking her back home, I took her to the steps of the *Chiesa di Sant'Andrea*, I went on my knees, and I proposed. I don't remember what I said, but I remember that I was shaking and I completely forgot the speech I had prepared. Just looking at her made me lose contact with the world around me. I wasn't surprised and thought I should have prepared better. That had happened so many times before. I told her I had forgotten my speech, but I said that I loved her immensely, that she was the most beautiful thing I had ever seen, and that I would give everything to keep waking up close to her for the rest of my life.

"She said 'yes,' and we married two weeks later, in that same church."

We had completed the "walls trail" once again, but kept walking. My father took only a few breaks from his story but anytime he did that, he didn't ask me questions or look for comments. He would just look at me as from a distance. I do believe at some point he became lost somewhere, somewhere far away from me. I kept holding his hand and listening to his story.

"I remember the night before we were ready to leave to go back to the U.S. She was eight months pregnant and could hardly move, although she kept organizing boxes and suitcases, making sure everything was ready to go. It was impossible to stop her. She insisted that I should not worry about her and that she was perfectly fine. She had refreshed her Italian and would sometimes mix English with Italian words."

"*Sono fine, non ti preoccupare*," she would say to me, smiling. I loved her smile.

"She was adorable." He took another break, and then there was some silence, but I didn't interrupt, and he continued.

"The flight to Connecticut went smoothly, but as soon as we landed, she started feeling bad, and went into labor. I was sure that, even if you were born a month early, there would be no problem. I tried to reassure her as we were heading to the hospital in a taxi. I didn't understand why she said that, and I was mad at her for doing so, but she made me promise that, if anything happened to her, I should marry again and make sure you had a mother who would take care of you as she would have. She also made me promise never to tell you about her unless you discovered her on your own. She said your name should be 'Clara,' and that she felt you were a girl.

"If I go back to those moments, I hate myself for being mad at her for what she was saying, for not holding her, for not living our last moments as I should have. As always, she knew what she was saying and she knew better than I did. She died in the delivery room because of an internal bleeding that nobody could have ever predicted and that could have easily killed both you and her. However, you did not die. You were put in an incubator, and I got to hold you in my arms soon after."

So my mother had died. Anna had died. I stopped walking, sat on the steps of a church, and started crying. Could not stop my tears. And I felt I was crying for Anna, for Joe, for my abandoned dreams, and for my life that had not made much sense until that moment. While my life was underwater, I had been swimming on the surface. I kept crying and at some point I could barely breathe. My father sat close to me and waited in silence. People around us were strolling and laughing, oblivious to our story, oblivious to us. Suddenly everything made no sense.

"I met Miriam a year later. I did not love her as I loved Anna, but she loved you, and you also seemed to like her. So I decided to give the three of us a chance. I told Miriam about Anna and my promise to her. She initially insisted that I tell you the truth as soon as you were old enough to understand. But as you grew up, she changed her mind and helped me keep my promise. She was maybe afraid that she could lose you, and I loved her for that.

"I've had much more time to know Miriam than I had to know Anna. She is a lovely person and she's been a wonderful mother to you. But I could never love anyone as I loved Anna. And that took me less than one day to know."

I abandoned my head to his shoulder, my hand in his hand. We stayed there until we were the only ones left. We remained silent, and although I could not say what he was thinking, I'm sure we were both thinking about Anna and asking why she died before either of us could truly know her.

Then I turned and I saw my father smiling.

"Do you want to know something?" he asked.

"What?"

"I think this is actually *Sant'Andrea*, the church where I proposed to Anna and where we got married."

I stood up, and opened my eyes wide to see. I turned and there it was, a beautiful, precious, old church. I turned again. That square, that church, reminded me of Monteriggioni. Perhaps that was why I liked it so much. Somehow it reminded me of something I hadn't seen, but felt I should have.

My father took my hand and asked me if I wanted to look inside. The door was open, and a priest was saying an evening mass for a small group of old women. We entered and walked silently along the side aisle, around the altar, and then to the other side of the church. That place was intimate and peaceful. I tried to imagine my mother and my father getting married there, happy and in love, and I felt happy for them, and sad for not having shared their love.

Before we left the church, I asked my father something I had not fully understood.

"You said Anna asked you to promise not to tell me about her unless I discovered her on my own. But I didn't."

"I think you did," he said. "You were looking for her. Your instinct was pushing you toward that woman who looked like you. I thought it was time for you to know. You needed that. This story is part of you, of the person you are, and the one you'll become. I'm sure Anna approves my choice."

He squeezed my hand.

"When I met your mother, my life became a magic, inexplicable dream, full of coincidences and events I could expect to read in fairy tales only. I stopped asking myself why things were happening to us. They just were. We were living a dream and the dream was our reality. Your questions about Joe and your search were asking if fairy tales are possible. I thought you should know that they are, and that you are part of one."

We walked home and I felt older, tired, but somehow released. Underwater. As soon as my head touched the pillow, I was asleep.

21

My visit with my father was perfect. We didn't do anything special, just walked and talked. Yes, we talked a lot, and I finally discovered him as a person and loved what I saw.

We spent our days talking about Anna and about love, and I finally understood his moods, his silences, his comments that sometimes seemed so distant from what I thought his life had been.

He brought some pictures with him and showed me a photo of their wedding, another one of Anna dancing flamenco, one where she was sitting at the piano, playing, and another where she held a painting she had just made. In that one, she was standing against a window, pregnant with me. She seemed happy, and I missed her. I miss her.

I always thought I looked more like my father than my mother, and often looked to him to understand parts of me that were unclear. Now that I had seen her though, I had seen me. There were so many things I wanted to ask her, and so I asked my father. Sometimes he could answer.

He told me about my mother's fears, stories that they

shared. At her core, she was art. Her life was. The dance, the piano, her cooking, her paintings.

He recalled how she loved to paint when they lived in Siena. He enjoyed watching her as she worked on a canvass propped on an easel, pressed against their living room window, because she needed to fly, as she said. She would put on music, dance while painting, and talk to the canvass as if it were alive. It would take her a few days to complete a painting. Then she said she was done and looked happy, almost relieved. I could see her, me doing that. But then, a day or so later, she would change her mind, tell him that, in fact, the painting wasn't finished at all, and leave the canvass on the floor in its unfinished limbo. Yes, I could see myself in there.

"I need to be inspired, Mark," she told him, when he asked her about a discarded painting she had not completed. And while waiting for her to be inspired again, their living room filled with temporarily finished, or not quite-so works, all waiting for her final touch. My father would then fake complaints, but he loved being surrounded by her passions and ideas, and she knew that.

He remembered her dancing flamenco in their apartment. She had taken lessons from a Spanish teacher and, from time to time, she would dance for my father, pulling him into a Spanish world she had made for the two of them. Right there. In their living room. I could see that.

"She wanted to be a professional dancer, and could have been. But she kept hearing the voices of her critics, and those voices became louder and louder, until she eventually believed them, and gave up. When you asked her about it, she said that the stage made her nervous. This is why she couldn't dance. Not professionally. That's what she said."

"Was she happy?" I asked.

"I think so. I hope she was. But I know she felt incomplete."

I thought about my fears, and wondered whether mine and hers were ungrounded. I would have asked her. I asked my father.

"You never insisted that I keep playing. You let me give up."

"I wasn't sure this is what you wanted. I guess we should have talked about it. It's probably my fault."

No, it wasn't his fault. I wanted to tell him that, tell him about Brussels, but decided not to. That now felt like an excuse, not a convincing one.

"You were an excellent pianist. But I worried that you might be playing for me. Listening to you playing was like having Anna in the room. You were growing up as an artist, pretty much like her, and that filled my heart. But I wanted you to find your own path in life, you had to decide for yourself. I liked your continuous search and dissatisfactions. You were, you are demanding, and I was confident that you would keep experimenting and finally choose the path that was best for you. I trusted you. I remember our chats about law school when you applied, your doubts and your interests. But once admitted, you did great and seemed to enjoy it. You seemed happy. Weren't you? Aren't you happy now?"

"I'm not sure."

"It's normal to have doubts and it's beautiful to keep looking. I suppose I'm still doing it myself." He paused, looked down, and then continued.

"It's possible you won't find all your answers. But you might find some. And they'll be good enough. Enough to keep you going. To keep you looking."

I thought about what he had just said and thought he was right.

I wrote a letter to Miriam, and asked my father to give it to her. In my letter, I told her how much I loved her, and how much I loved her for loving me the way she did, without limit or condition. And I thanked her for helping my father keep his promise to Anna. I was sure that must not have been easy.

My father's meeting with Mario was a chance meeting near the door to my building. I had told Mario about Anna, and he said he wanted me to spend time alone with my father. When they met, they hugged as old friends. Mario said we looked happy and, indeed, we were.

And then my father left. I took him to the airport and made him promise he would return soon. He said he would, and I believed him. I knew there was more for us to explore.

I had only one week before resuming work, and that seemed not enough. There was so much unresolved in my life. I needed time.

"What about talking to my boss and asking for more time off?" I asked Mario.

"Do you really think one or two more weeks would fix you?"

He was right. Even a few extra weeks would not be enough. And they needed me to start working on the new Downing projects. If I had asked for more time, someone else would be put in charge and, most likely, I would have to return to L.A.

"You don't need to keep your job to stay in Siena or anywhere else in Italy," Mario said, somehow reading my mind.

"Of course I do. I need money to live."

"I understand," he insisted, "but you don't necessarily need *that* job to make money. You could do something else. Shouldn't you be an Italian citizen?"

I had not thought about that. He might be right. My mother was Italian. I should be too.

"But doesn't it take time, perhaps a long time, to become a citizen?"

He left his living room and returned with a consumed pocket phone book. He leafed through it and made a phone call.

"*Franco, ho bisogno di un passaporto italiano da fare in fretta. Mi puoi aiutare*?"

Mario never stopped surprising me. He had a friend at the Italian Consulate in Los Angeles, and this friend told him how he could request and quickly obtain an Italian passport for me. He took notes, thanked his friend, and hung up.

"Here's what they need." He showed me a list of documents that were seemed easy to collect.

"You could have your passport in two or three weeks," he said. "My friend will help us expedite the procedure, if needed."

I was shocked. I was going to get my Italian passport, and that would allow me to work in Italy.

"But if I quit, what will I do?" I asked him, hoping he would know that too.

"You should tell me that."

Yes, I should have, but I felt lost, disoriented, and scared. I was renouncing something as safe and secure as my job, one I'd spent years training for, in exchange for nothing. But why was I a lawyer and not a pianist or a baker or something else? I had to figure that out. I didn't want to settle for the surface again. I had to keep looking underwater. After all, I had just started. I knew there was much more out there.

I called Elizabeth and told her that I had decided to quit.

She was speechless. I apologized for that news, I knew they had counted on me, and I was thankful for their support and trust. I said something crucial had happened, and I needed time to process it. I don't know if she understood. She wished me good luck, and I was free to go. My eyes wide open.

I told Mario about my decision and he said he was proud of me. My parents were less enthusiastic, but they were supportive. They asked me what I was going to do, if I had plans. I said I didn't, but strangely, everything finally looked just fine.

22

I had savings, but I needed to budget carefully, and find a less expensive place to stay. Mario offered me a room in his place, but I thought I should be on my own.

One day, as I was walking close to *Sant'Andrea*, I decided to visit that church. It was early afternoon and the church was empty. I thought I could sit there and talk to Anna or simply talk to myself. I recalled what Mario had said in the *Pantheon*. Silencing the noise would make me see things more clearly. The silent solitude of that church worked.

I thought about what to do, where to start, and I decided it would make sense to walk around the city and look for an apartment to rent. I didn't pray, I didn't know how to, but I asked Anna, if she could hear me, to help me stay in Siena. I really didn't want to leave.

It was August, it was hot, and the city seemed deserted. The students had left after taking their last exams, and everyone or almost everyone seemed to be away, vacationing somewhere. I thought it might be hard to find a room to rent at that time, but when I left the church, on *Via della Stufa*

Secca, I saw a sign that read "*Affittasi a studenti.*" There was a phone number and I called.

The landlady said the apartment had four rooms, three of which had been rented to students who would return in the fall. If I was a student and interested in seeing the apartment, she could show it to me now.

The apartment was close by, and we met in front of it before I could even realize it. It was modern but inviting. The hardwood floor and the big windows brightened a wide living room. And there were many chairs around a big table. I could see parties taking place right there. One perhaps a few days before everyone left.

She showed me the other students' rooms and explained that they had gone home for the summer. The rooms were not too big, but big enough to have some space and comfort. I noticed that there was a drum kit in one of them, which basically took up most of the room. She must have noticed that I was surprised to see a set of drums, and asked whether that bothered me.

"No, not at all," I replied, and then, to my own surprise, I told her that I was studying piano and would bring one there. If that was O.K.

"You are the perfect tenant," she said. "The boys are all musicians."

I gave her a check for the deposit that same afternoon, and the room was mine. A young friend of Mario's helped me move, and the move was complete by *ferragosto*, August 15. I had even rented a piano.

The last two weeks of August were fabulous. I had the full apartment to myself, and spent my days playing, going for walks, and sharing meals and ideas with Mario. He came for dinner almost every night, and we talked about the blessings of having no plans, but if I grew anxious, he gave me the nudges I needed. We talked about Clara less and less. I had yet to absorb the news of my mother and found myself thinking of Anna more than I did of Clara. But I did think about Clara, from time to time, and told myself I would resume that search one day. Just didn't know when.

"Are you frightened?" Mario asked me once.

"Frightened of what?"

"Of your future."

I said that I was, but that I was more excited than scared. I could be a new person, change the things in my life I didn't like, find a true path. And I believed it. All of it.

The last day of August, as I was finishing baking a cake, I heard a key in the latch. I jumped. I thought it might be a burglar. I had completely forgotten that I was sharing the apartment with someone else. It was, in fact, one of my roommates, Andrea. He was twenty-six and had just graduated from the Conservatory of Roma. He was the drummer.

"Hi, you must be the pianist," he said in perfect English, as he ducked in through the door. "You're American, right?"

"Yes, I am. I'm Clara."

"Ciao Clara, pleasure to meet you. I was excited when I heard that you played piano. This is such a great coincidence. We're all musicians here. I play the drums, Paolo plays bass, and Renato, the trumpet. We initially hooked up to form a group, and then moved in together."

"That sounds nice," I smiled. "I'm not a professional," I then added, trying to lower his expectations and keep some distance.

"What do you mean by 'professional'?" he asked. "You're studying piano, no? How can you study piano 'unprofessionally'? If you are studying piano, you are a professional."

"I actually *did* study piano. I studied at a conservatory for a while but dropped out years ago."

"I see. And what are you studying now?"

I thought about telling him the truth, that I was a lawyer, that I had worked for this big law firm and so on, but then changed my mind.

"Let's say I'm taking a break from work, and I'm planning to fill my days with music and some good reads. In fact, this is pretty much what I've been doing lately."

He didn't ask more questions, and just said that he and the guys played jazz, and it would be nice if I would join them sometimes.

I smiled and said I would think about it.

"Did you make that?" he then asked, pointing to the chocolate cake that was resting on the stove.

"Yes, I did."

"May I try it? I'm starving."

"Of course."

I was happy to have someone in the house, and happy that someone was him.

I liked Andrea. He was enthusiastic and a little crazy. A drummer. And I liked Paolo and Renato too when I met them only a few days later. They were older. Paolo was thirty and Renato thirty-two. Andrea was the extrovert, Paolo the introvert. That seemed common among bass players, I thought. Renato was more natural and open, but not like Andrea, clearly the go-go person of the group. Renato also loved cooking and was an *esperto* of red wines, as he used to describe himself. He was fun and incredibly intelligent.

Paolo didn't say much. He observed people and everything around him, immersed in his own thoughts most of the time. He had recently broken up with his girlfriend, Marivì, and spent time in his room playing and composing songs for her, or going for long walks around the city, sometimes disappearing for hours and coming home semi-drunk.

"He'll be fine, don't worry," Renato told me once. "He and Marivì have broken up so many times since we know him, and every time he goes through this. And before you can even say, they're back together. And then they break up again."

All my roommates spoke English and wanted to improve, so we spoke English almost always, except at dinner or lunch, when it was harder for them to talk about food and ingredients without gesturing in Italian and singing or something like that. Also they said their food had an Italian soul, and speaking English while having a meal would be like betraying or offending it. I never understood that, but I thought they were fun, and I took our meals as my time to practice Italian. And I was happy to practice with them, even if they constantly teased me for my accent, especially when I said "*cioccolato.*" I couldn't resist using that word or perhaps hearing them laugh at me for the way I did. We got along very well, and I loved them.

They practiced for hours, usually in Andrea's room, repeating this or that arrangement a thousand times. I understood that. I did it myself. Repeat and repeat and repeat. Only musicians know what that means, and understand and respect anyone engaged in the art of perfecting art. So no, it didn't bother me.

They always asked me to join, and I always refused. "I'm not ready yet," was my standard reply. I practiced only when I was alone so nobody could hear, and I was alone often, as everyone had jobs or classes and was away most of the day.

One day, when I thought everyone had left, I pulled the *Gymnopédies* and started playing. I had not played them in years, and was so excited that I forgot to check and see whether I was truly alone. I hesitated a bit on the first notes, but then played those three pieces as if I had never stopped.

I was so immersed in that music that I didn't notice Paolo was there, sitting just behind me. When I finished playing and rose from my seat, I saw him and tried to catch my breath without making him notice. But I think he did.

"What are you...? How long have you been here?"

He smiled.

"So that's you. Interesting. I'm sorry. I know you don't like people hearing you play, but I couldn't help it."

"It's fine. I'm sorry if I woke you up or bothered you," I said, moving my sheet music and pretending it wasn't a big deal.

"Bother me? What would bother me?"

I was still out of breath, so I sat down, and tried to catch my thoughts. He rose, and went to the kitchen.

"Coffee?"

"Yes, thanks," I said, waiting for him to say more, although I couldn't exactly anticipate what that could be. Paolo and I had not spoken that much.

"It's beautiful to hear you play. It's like meeting you for the first time," he said, and handed me the coffee. He poured some coffee for himself, and disappeared into his room.

I remained seated at my piano for a while, thinking of what he had just said. I wished I had the courage to continue playing, but I didn't. Someone had entered my silence and I felt almost violated. Bad for what had just happened, and bad for sensing that sharing as an intrusion. I took a shower, closed my eyes, and cried under that rain. The Roman fountain a far memory. My silence, one that had never left me.

I left the apartment and wandered around Siena. It was September and there was a nice, late summer breeze. As I was thinking about Paolo's words, I found myself close to the city walls, and started walking along them, as I had done with my father. And as it had happened with him, I soon lost contact with the city and the people around me, floating between memories of mine and my parents' past. I thought about Anna, my father's description of her, and her story became mine, or mine hers. It was me dancing, me playing, I was in Siena, I had met people, I had made friends, I was afraid, I made excuses.

I continued to walk, and after two or three trips along the walls, I felt as if the spiral I had created with my wandering had swallowed my past and Anna's, and mixed the two together. And the mix was so perfect that there were no longer two stories. Just one. I hoped I could continue that story without making the same mistakes she, or I, or both had made.

23

September went by fast. I spent my days taking long walks with Mario, reading, and playing Ravel. I still didn't feel comfortable playing when everyone was around, but now it didn't bother me if Paolo was there, as I had upgraded him to silent spectator, no longer an intruder.

He would come to my room with a book, sit on the floor, and read as I played. He wouldn't say a word, not a single comment on my music. He would just sit, read, and when I was done playing, leave.

Renato and Andrea had not heard me play yet, and they had become increasingly curious.

"C'mon, Clara," Andrea pressed one day. "It has been more than a month since we met, and we haven't heard a note from you."

"I'm not..."

"Yes, we know. You are not ready. But when will you be?" Renato nodded in agreement, looking for Paolo's support. But Paolo didn't say a word. He looked to his plate, then at me, and smiled. We had a secret.

William arrived at the end of September. When I went to

the airport to pick him up, I barely recognized him. He had gained weight, grown his beard, and looked older. He was completing his residency at a children's hospital in Connecticut and blamed what I saw on the cafeteria and his stress.

"But look at you, Smith. You haven't changed at all." He took my right hand and turned me in a circle.

"Except for the hair. Wow, that's big. What happened?"

I smiled, hugged him, and something, my memories, the good ones, came back. We remained sealed. His bags on the floor of the arrival platform, while passengers were trying to navigate around them and us. Time stopped right there. It seemed to last forever. And yet, if I could, I would have made it last longer. I wanted to say I was sorry for the time lost, but I didn't.

I took his hand, and dragged him to the car. I asked him about his trip, his experience at the hospital, and he said he wanted a full report on what had happened to me during these years. I told him that not much had happened. Just a law degree and some law firm experience. I explained why I was in Siena, and when he asked me when I thought I would go back to the U.S., I said I didn't know and had no plans.

"Of course you don't. Smith hates plans. She improvises, right?"

There was some resentment in his voice, or perhaps just his idea that my lack of plans was my childish dream or my childish inability to commit to anything. Was he mad at me for that? Disappointed? Jealous?

If I had been given an opportunity to go back, I would have done things differently. I hadn't talked enough about myself with him. I had mostly listened. And yes, I had played for him, but not that often. So what did he really know about me? I wished I had spoken more, and I wished we had asked each other all the questions that were crossing our minds. I wondered how our life would have been if we had done that, if we had been totally honest with each other. We had probably missed something important, and I felt sorry for us.

I always thought friends would tell each other everything. I thought this made them different from the rest of the world, and from lovers too. But we hadn't told each other everything. And we weren't lovers either. So what were we really? I didn't even have a preference for one or the other label. I just needed to know, as I felt confused about us. I always had. And maybe that had wrecked most of my decisions. Joe and my career included.

I used to look underwater, I couldn't avoid that, but what happened between me and William had made me stop. It wasn't Brussels, really. I could see things more clearly now. It was us, and the thought that I had been wrong about us, that I had missed something. So why bother looking? I would be wrong again. I could be.

But had I ever explored our relationship? The part of it that was underwater? The one you would miss if you stopped at the surface? Maybe I never had. And it wasn't lack of interest. Perhaps it was lack of capacity, love and fear of being wrong.

Meanwhile, he had decided about us. He seemed to. And he must have been right. Right about everything. As my memories now looked like a castle of thoughts and assumptions, one that I had myself built. I might have concluded I'd been wrong in assessing things I had never even seen. So if I had been wrong about my feelings for him and his feelings for me, something that I felt so strong, maybe I could be wrong on anything else. Music. Law. Joe.

I felt unresolved, and mad at myself for not having fought, for not having tried harder. Should I try now? Would I be able to?

"And you? How is it going?" I asked, trying to pull those questions and their pins from my brain. I needed relief. "Are you seeing anyone?" I asked.

"Yes." He paused, and turned to search my eyes.

No, that wasn't exactly the right choice. My question to him wasn't.

"I've been seeing this girl for three years now. She's very smart." He showed me one of their close-ups. They were hugging each other.

"Oh," I said. "Nice."

Were they as close as they looked? Had she replaced me? This is what I wanted to ask. Instead I asked him her name.

"Katie. Her name's Katie. She's a doctor, and she has a Ph.D. from Yale. Also plays piano. Like you. You know I have always had a thing for pianists."

Really? No, I didn't know. He never told me that. Was he joking?

"She'll join me later this week," he continued. "We'll spend a few days in Florence and then go to the Amalfi Coast. She'll be the perfect guide. She reads a lot and is a great planner."

"Like you," I said.

"Right. And unlike you."

"Florence and the Amalfi Coast. Sounds romantic, important."

"Yeah. Actually, it's supposed to be our pre-wedding honey-moon."

I felt like someone or something had just sucked my stomach. All of it. I tried not to show it, but my attempt was pathetic.

"You're getting married?"

"Yes. Can you believe it?"

No, I could not.

"So she's the one?"

"Yes, yes. She's a wonderful doctor. Very smart. I respect her. I'm sure she'll be a great mother to my kids. I hope we'll have many. Four, maybe. You never wanted kids, right?"

"I...."

I never thought about kids. But why that question? And why that comparison? Wasn't I supposed to be his best friend?

"That's great," I said. "I'm happy for you."

He smiled and remained silent for a while, looking outside the window of my car as we passed through the countryside. I would have given everything to know what he was thinking right at that moment, or to just be brave enough to push him against the wall of his plans and show him how empty and pathetic they sometimes were, but I didn't. I wasn't brave enough. Or perhaps I was afraid to find out that the only pathetic thing in there was my romantic idea about us and my improvisations.

Meanwhile, he was getting married.

As I was driving, from time to time, and when he didn't notice, I looked at him and tried to understand what had I missed of him. I thought about asking him a forward question, but as I was playing with alternatives in my mind, he spoke.

"I know what you're thinking."

"Really? What am I thinking?" I asked, as if I were asking that question to a fortune-teller on the street to test his ability, hoping he would be right.

"You're wondering how I managed to finally commit to someone. Is that right?"

No, it wasn't right. But he thought it was, and I didn't want to disappoint him. My disappointment being enough. For both of us.

"I knew it. You're an open book to me, Smith."

I wished I was. That would have made everything easier.

"It wasn't easy, and she was patient with me. She's very smart, you know," he continued.

Right, I got that, and I was tired of hearing it over and over again. She was smart. She was a doctor. She had a Ph.D. It was as if he had picked her through an application process and a check-list, all carefully designed by him. The Ph.D. and her IQ on top of his list. Perhaps her scores too. I wasn't surprised. That was him. And that should have been enough to turn off my feelings. Instead, I felt more.

I felt the same distance I had felt from time to time, when he would hurt me and I wouldn't tell him, when he tried hard to convince me and himself that my romantic idea of love was nothing but a fantasy, and I gave up, exhausted after hours of confrontation with him on that topic. "It's a partnership," he would say, "a partnership for success. You build it over the years. You don't fall in love with your eyes and your heart. The heart doesn't have feelings. Everything starts from your brain, Smith." I could still hear his voice. I wondered if he ever believed what he said, and I wished I had asked him.

When he went to med school, during his first semester, there were times when he would call me late at night, almost every night, and keep me on the phone for hours. It was as if there was always something we absolutely needed to discuss, something that couldn't wait. It was either a movie we both saw, or a book we both read, an article, something. His phone calls said "I can't sleep and I miss you." And I missed him too. But sometimes I wished he hadn't called. Sometimes I wished he'd let me alone to make me understand what we really had and what we were. What we had and what we were when we were apart. To understand, I needed silence. To understand, he needed to talk things through, without even naming them, almost leaving them in a safe background. Or at least, this is how it felt. And so he called and called, and when he did, I felt his solitude, and did my best to breathe in some peace through the distance and that cheap receiver. How naïve of me to think that I could do that? But I did. Sometimes I succeeded, and I felt so happy when I did.

We were bonded together, more than we knew, more than we were aware of. But sometimes that felt just absurd. Too out of the ordinary to be true. So one night, after a three-hour call, when he had finally started to fall asleep, I wanted to ask him whether we were in love. At that time, I was at peace with myself and my feelings, and that would have been just an honest question from a friend to another. But I didn't ask. That question had remained unanswered, and I still had it. Too bad. Now it would be harder to ask. We hadn't had an intimate conversation in so many years. And he was now getting married, and I might wreck his perfect plan, one where I was his best friend, in good times and in bad, in sickness and in health. The marriage he had asked for, the one I had not.

"I'll be there," I said. "Even if I'm still in Siena, I'll come to your wedding. I promise."

That's all I said. And I thought about Paolo and what he said when he heard me play Satie. He said that hearing me play felt like meeting me for the first time, as if I could be honest only when I played. If I could be myself only through my music, did anyone really know me? Did William know me? And if he did, did he forget or lose me when I stopped playing? And why did I stop playing really? Didn't I want to be myself? At least for myself? Did I stop being interested in myself because I decided William wasn't?

"When will the wedding be?" I asked. "And where?"

"July, next year. In L.A. That's where she grew up."

"Sure, I'll be there. I've an apartment there."

He looked at me as if he wanted to know more, but I said he should rest and take a nap as I drove. We would soon be at my place, and the guys were preparing a welcome dinner for him and, I was sure, more questions than he could handle. He would need energy.

He replied that he was fine, but when I turned on the radio, he closed his eyes, surrendered to the back of the seat, and fell asleep. He drifted off, and I drifted into my thoughts.

When we arrived at the apartment, I parked Andrea's car and woke William up. The guys were all waiting for us, making dinner. I smelled Renato's fresh tomato sauce from the street, and William did too.

"We're in Italy. That totally makes sense," he said, taking a look around.

"What does?"

"The smell of fresh food in the street, and you being here."

"Why do you say so?"

"I don't know. Just a feeling."

Did he know me?

The guys and William clicked immediately. They talked about football and famous Italian baseball players, about William's experience in the hospital, his travel plans, his wedding. They told him about their music and complained that I wouldn't play with them.

"She's awesome," William said. "She's played piano since she was three or four. All over the world. Everywhere."

"No, that's not true. I just did a couple of concerts overseas."

He told them about the pieces I played, of how everyone in our class thought I was going to become this famous pianist. He said that everyone feared me, that they thought I was a little genius in her own world, that I didn't talk to anyone, anyone except him. He said I had picked him as a friend and looked proud. In fact, he had picked me, and I was proud too.

William told them more about my music and my concerts, and then Andrea said they would kick me out of the house if I didn't agree to play at least once with them.

"Why don't you play *Take Five*?" William pressed, looking at me.

"I don't think I can. I haven't played it in forever. I'm not even sure I remember it."

"I'm sure you do," he said. "You played it often, too often to have forgotten. Do you remember when you played it for me?"

Yes, I did. Of course I did. I had played *Take Five* for him so many times. He loved that piece and would beg me to play it when he was sad. He said it made him happy, and indeed it seemed to work.

After some pressure, and some more wine, I surrendered. I'm not sure why, though. It wasn't my curiosity, the need to test my memory, my ability, or my performance with the guys. And it wasn't that all of a sudden it seemed easy to play for someone other than myself. It was still hard. It felt hard. But maybe I wanted William to see me, see the person that I was, not the one that had been silent in the car or the many times before. I wanted him to see the person who felt, the one who dreamt, the one who loved. Me. I wanted him to see me again.

And so I played, we did, and I was surprised. Surprised we could play so well together without even rehearsing once, and surprised that I remembered that piece. The pace was perfect, we had a great chemistry, and the guys insisted that I join their group. I smiled, but didn't discard that possibility completely. Maybe it was the wine.

When it was about midnight and I had finished washing the dishes, I asked William if he wanted to go for a walk.

"I'll show you Siena. It'll be deserted at this time, but perhaps even more fascinating than during the day."

He agreed, and we left.

The night was warm, and the streets were empty canvasses filled with life possibilities. We would have to pick one, draw one.

"So what's up?" he asked, as if we hadn't talked before.

"You said you quit your job?"

"Right. I did. I wasn't happy."

"Why?"

"I felt I had to control myself too often, think about what to say and when, make sure it fit one of the boxes I was given. Please this or that partner, this or that associate. Do politics. You know I'm not good at that."

"You are a great lawyer."

"How do you know?" I asked. "Was that another of your plans for me?"

This time I had spoken, but my voice had been too loud, almost off-key. Was it the wine or the music?

"What? I don't get it."

"I always felt you had a plan for me, one I had to fit into not to disappoint you. Law was one of them, wasn't it?"

"What are you talking about? You didn't even talk to me when you decided to apply to law school."

"I didn't because I felt there was no need. You kept saying that was how you saw me. Your lawyer friend. I thought that was what ought to be."

I had actually never thought about what I had just said. My interest in law had always looked like a mystery to me. But now it didn't seem so. It all started to make sense. Was it the music that suggested that?

"We were joking, I was joking with you. You loved to argue, you were, you are smart. I thought it made sense. But becoming a lawyer was your choice, Clara, not mine. And it was your choice to give up on piano too. You were great in Brussels. You thought it was a failure. You didn't even want to read the papers. Your critics were beyond words. I was too young to know how to help you, and you were too. But we never talked about it. Remember, you didn't want to. You were so locked into yourself that anytime you revealed something about you it sounded almost a mistake."

He took a deep breath.

"When I called you, and we talked for hours, I was hoping I could make you tired enough to open you up. But you rarely did. And when after two or three hours I would finally give up, I felt I had failed again. You had not shared enough about yourself. But I wouldn't give up. I would try again, wait, and then try some more. I did try. Until you let me."

So that's what it was?

"I wanted to talk about our relationship, but I wasn't trustworthy, I knew I wasn't. I would have not trusted myself. So I was waiting for you to say something, to convince me that I could be with you. But you never did. You just ran away."

"But that Christmas..."

"Yes, that Christmas I was an idiot. When we kissed, I felt scared and confused. I went to that party, and I did meet someone. But nothing happened."

"But Matt...?"

"He asked me about it and I didn't know what to say. I was thinking of you and felt terrible. I didn't want him to know, and I made up a story, one of my usual. Except it wasn't true."

I started shaking. All those years....

"I tried to call you, but you wouldn't answer the phone. And what was I supposed to tell you? That I loved you? I didn't know if I did. But mostly, I was afraid I could hurt you. So I let you decide about us. And then, when you texted me after months, and you confessed that you were attracted to me, I had suffered too much, and thought it was better if you and I remained best friends. You and I together seemed really too complicated for me to be able to handle."

I looked into his eyes. We were underwater. *Piazza del Campo* was. We sat on the bricks and he continued.

"I had feelings for you. But how could you expect me to commit to them? You knew me. I couldn't hold any of my promises. You were the one who kept our promises for us. I didn't want to hurt you. Tell you about my feelings and then what? Convince you that you felt the same? And then what? Betray them? Betray you? I waited and waited for us to solve this, but we never did. I found a girlfriend, then another one, and then another one. And they all looked like you."

He pulled the photo of his fiancé and showed it to me. Yes, I could see the resemblance. She was thin, pale, short, and her glasses seemed to speak about someone more interested in her books than in the outside world. Just like me.

"You know what the sad part of this is?"

I remained silent.

He looked at me but didn't answer his question.

He then checked the time, and said we'd better go. There weren't enough canvasses for us to draw our feelings in there. There just weren't enough.

24

When we got home, William crashed on the living room couch. I made some tea and went to my room. I sat on the piano bench and leafed through pages of memories I wished I had written. I saw my castle of assumptions and entered. It looked tall and empty now, and I could hear my silence laughing at me. Again.

I turned to my piano and looked at the stack of sheet music. Ravel, Debussy, Chopin, Lizst, Rachmaninoff, De Falla, Mussorgsky, Brahms.... I spread the music on the floor and remembered.

I saw the notes I had written on the margins, the numbers I had assigned to each finger, the breathing signs. And I could see the dim light illuminating that music when it was late, the nights spent playing and thinking, the stains of coffee to keep me awake. I saw that world again and I missed it.

In all those years, my music had been the most truthful thing I had. And true, I had interpreted it as I had interpreted William, Brussels, and so many other things in my life. But I had gotten my music right. Perhaps Brussels had been right too. It scared me, but it might have been right.

I pulled the *Mephisto Waltz* and played and replayed it in my head, practicing with my fingers on the sheet music, trying this or that passage over and over. My consumed pages working as my keyboard.

It was morning, but it was still dark, and silent. The music my fingers were mimicking was loud, but only I could hear it. And then I played the *Waltz* on my iPod and played it in my head following the music.

When the sun rose, I made a cake, brewed some coffee, and when everyone was awake, I said I had something I wanted to show them. I asked them to come to my room and sit on my bed and when I brought them cake and coffee, they smiled and thanked me for the surprise.

"That's actually not it," I said, opened my piano, and played the *Mephisto Waltz*.

I made a couple of mistakes here and there, but the music was there. Most of it was. I was there though. Completely. And the music was so loud that, slowly, the sound hit the walls of my castle and they crashed.

When I finished playing, everyone remained silent, as if they had witnessed something big they were not expecting. The castle was on the floor. I turned toward them and smiled. My music had just introduced me to them.

Paolo smiled. There was some silence, and then everyone applauded.

25

William and I spent a few days wandering around Siena. I told him about Mario, and showed him many of the places Mario had showed me. I also told him about Anna and what my father had told me. He asked me how I felt and I said I felt happier than I had felt in many years, as I was swimming underwater again, and things had started to make sense.

"I think this is what I always liked about you."

"What?"

"You always gave me a feeling of someone submerged. You were always a mystery to me. And I wanted to come find you."

Yes, things had started to make sense.

I told him about Mario's photo, Clara, and our search.

"You were clearly looking for your mother," he said, when I finished my story.

"Really? How so?"

"I wouldn't have not gone on a trip looking for my double. People have doubles. It happens. And it can happen that they share more than their appearances. But going on a trip looking for them? You'd do that only if you felt there was something else you were looking for. Don't you think?"

I thought he was right, and realized that my father had indeed not broken his promise to Anna.

"But now that you have started, you shouldn't stop it."

"What do you mean?"

"You met all these people, collected all this information about her. I feel you're close to finding her. And if I were you, I'd keep looking."

"And what would you do?" I asked.

"I'd go to Firenze and look for her there. You have the address of her parents, right? We could go there together."

"Aren't you supposed to visit Firenze with Katie?"

"Yes, I am, and I will. But I'd like to go there with you. It'll be like in the good old days."

I liked the idea, and even if I had somehow lost interest in that search now, I felt it would be fun to go.

We took a train that morning, and soon we were in Firenze. It was late morning and the train station was packed. I pulled the address of Clara's parents from my pocket and a map with directions to that place. I asked William if he wanted to tour the city first, but he said we should start with Clara, and so we did.

Clara's or her parents' address was "Piazza de' Pitti, 12." It was a nice walk from the station and to get there we passed through beautiful alleys filled with boutiques, café, restaurants with tables shaky on the cobblestone, and flower shops. We walked, immersed in the sun and the stone buildings that seemed to tell stories of an elegant past. I thought it would have been nice to have lived those times too.

"Why do we have one life only?" I asked William at some point.

"Why would you want more?"

"To live different times and come back to the present with more experience, wisdom. For fun. For art."

He smiled, grabbed my hand and we walked on *Ponte Vecchio*, losing ourselves somewhere on that Medieval stone bridge over the Arno River, among jewelers, art dealers, souvenir sellers, and love stories. The one we could see. And the ones we couldn't. It was enchanting.

"There's a legend here," he said, showing me what seemed a wall of shackled padlocks.

"What is it?" I asked. "And why all these padlocks?"

"The legend says that if you're in love with someone and chain a padlock together with that person anywhere on the Old Bridge, and then throw the key into the river, your love will live forever."

"Oh," I said. "I get why you wanted to take Katie here."

He pulled his padlock from his pocket, and looked at it. Then looked up. I remembered that look. I had seen it only once, that night we kissed. And it hadn't changed at all. Had I been wrong about us?

"What?" I asked.

"Do you want to do it?"

I remained silent. He pressed my hand in his, and with the other, locked the padlock to a chain on the bridge and then handed me the key.

I took it, looked at it, and threw it in the river. But I knew I wasn't making a wish for us. I was just sealing what it had always been. And there, underwater, where everything looked out of focus, softer, and less defined than in real life, less logic, we found each other.

"Ready?" he then asked.

"I think I am," I said, and was thankful to him for making me so.

Piazza de' Pitti was a short walk from the bridge. It was

majestic, and the art of *Palazzo Pitti* seemed to have escaped the museum and spread across the square. When we got to the middle of the *piazza*, I closed my eyes and heard a music I thought I should write.

"What are you thinking?"

"I'm thinking that I'd like to write about this?"

"About what?"

I smiled.

"You'll know when you hear it."

"Here," William then said, dragging me to a slender, old building, almost pressed between other two that were perhaps as old but more lively.

"This is it," he said.

I checked and he was right. That was Piazza de' Pitti, 12.

I looked up trying to spot some life in that building, but I didn't. The shutters were mostly closed, but those that were open were so old that they seemed to be ready to fall any moment. There was a little shop on the ground floor, though, and that was open. Antíc Art. That was its name. We entered and waited for someone to show up.

We had been there for a while, and had shouted *buon giorno* two or three times already, but nobody appeared. We didn't leave.

The store was a little storage of memories and stories. Old chairs and nightstands, a consumed desk that had perhaps belonged to a writer or a scientist, a lamp that looked tired of holding its light, iron, dried flowers in dusty vases, a child's crib, paintings that could have been worth a fortune or a couple of bucks, but I couldn't say, and photos of a distant time. The past seemed to have invaded the store leaving no space for the present. Or perhaps the present would just not fit there.

It seemed there was no one attending to the store. But

someone must have. So we waited and finally a man showed up. He was old, perhaps in his nineties. His name was Peppe, and the store was his own. He was so happy to see us. He said he didn't have customers often. I thought he might have had, but perhaps he just hadn't seen them or heard them. He didn't speak English, except for numbers, amounts, conversions, and the most basic customer-seller word repertoire. So I used my Italian and perhaps impressed William.

I asked him about the Bassi family. He said they no longer lived there. He said Clara's parents had died many years earlier, and their daughter had never come back. Or at least, he had not seen her in many years. He didn't know where she was and if she was still alive. But he hoped she was, as she was special, he said. Yes, that sounded like Clara. I believed that man and his story. He looked like someone who had spent his entire life in Firenze and his store. Someone loyal to the past. Someone to believe.

So we hadn't found Clara, or her parents, but I seemed to see things more clearly every day. There, underwater.

"Are you disappointed?" William asked when we left.

I smiled. No, I wasn't disappointed. I was happy, and I felt he knew that.

We walked more and saw beautiful *piazzas*, churches, statutes, improvised markets on the streets or in alleys, and an official one, *Mercato Centrale*, with displays of Tuscan cuisine, fresh fish, fruits, nuts, vegetables. We lost ourselves in that mix of scents and colors, grabbed some of that for lunch, and kept walking and talking.

We talked about my years in law school, the law firm, my struggles, and the things that I liked. I confessed that I had met someone before coming to Italy, but that I had been too confused to continue that relationship.

"Why?" he asked.

I looked at him, and thought about the key we had thrown in the river.

"I think it was you."

He hugged me, and we continued to walk, silently. I didn't know what he was thinking, but for the first time, I didn't need to know.

"Do you love him?"

"I'll find out," I said.

He turned, and looked somewhere, and let my hand go. But it felt as he never left it. We had thrown the key in the river. Our hands had been sealed.

We wandered a bit more, without direction or plans, more my way than his, but he seemed to enjoy it, even if sometimes we returned to streets and places we had already seen.

And then I saw a street sign that said *Fountain of Neptune.* I thought about the Trevi Fountain and told William I wanted to see that. He agreed, and we walked there.

The fountain was in *Piazza della Signoria*, in front of the *Palazzo Vecchio*, a beautiful building with a little tower that seemed to have combined the *Palazzo Pubblico* and the *Torre del Mangia* in Siena. So Firenze had some of Siena and some of Roma, but here the building was *Vecchio*, not of the public but of the *signori*, and Neptune was at peace, or at least he seemed so, more than in Roma. Would people throw coins in his fountain? I had no wishes to express. I closed my eyes and thanked something or someone for feeling the way I did.

When it was late, we took the train and returned to Siena. On the train, we hugged and fell asleep. I freed my thoughts, my silences and my dreams. I sat on them and watched us. I loved what I saw.

26

William slept most of the next day. He woke up in the evening and we went to dinner with Mario. After dinner, we went to Mario's place and he showed William some of his photos and stories. I didn't know that William had developed a passion for photography. He paused on the details of Mario's photos, and explained to me, and perhaps to Mario too, why he thought they were exceptional.

We spent hours leafing through Mario's files, discussing about this or that detail, the light, the shadows, the stories Mario had written. But at some point I noticed that both William and Mario were getting tired, so I asked Mario to play one of his jazz LPs on his gramophone, and the three of us danced to that music.

When Mario was in the kitchen pouring each of us a glass of wine, William called me to the hall. There were some prints he wanted to show me.

"Do you know this artist?" he asked.

I shook my head.

"Masahisa Fukase. You see these ravens?" he said,

pointing at a print showing a man's face, his eyes closed, surrounded by ravens. "The ravens are his dark thoughts. They're attacking his mind."

"That's intense," I said, and examined the photos carefully, from different angles. They seemed almost tridimensional. How did he do that?

"Yeah. It's amazing. You can feel his isolation. In Japanese mythology, ravens foretell dark and dangerous times. I love his art. It really speaks to me."

Did it? Why? When I was about to ask him, Mario came with the wine.

"You like Fukase?" Mario asked.

"Yes, very much," William said, "this one overwhelms me."

"I know," Mario said, and the two exchanged a look that seemed to share more than what they had just said.

We drank the wine and listened to more music. It was getting late, and so at some point I suggested that we leave. William and Mario hugged.

"Make sure you don't lose this precious thing again," Mario said to William, pointing at me. "It would be a waste."

William smiled and looked at me.

"And promise me you'll take good care of her," Mario added.

"I will, Mario. I promise."

When we went home, we went to bed, and I fell asleep right away. But at some point I thought I heard William say something. I don't remember all of it as I was sleeping. But I think he said that he was happy I had found Mario, as Mario reminded him of himself when he would get older.

That night I dreamt of seagulls falling in love with ravens.

The next day, when I took William to the train station, it

was hard to say good-bye. Seemed too soon. I hugged him, and held him tight. I didn't want to let him go. Tears stained my face.

"I'll miss you Smith."

I smiled, watched him slowly disappear behind the sliding doors, and when I turned to walk back to my car, the fall came.

27

The fall came and went, and I turned twenty-nine. Music filled my days. I practiced every day, all day, sometimes on my own, sometimes with the guys, with few breaks.

Mario and I would meet on the weekends, but sometimes also during the week. We had started working on his stories again, but not with the same intensity as before. We would take long walks, and on some nights we went back to Monteriggioni, mostly to chat and be part of that peaceful beauty, now ready to offer some of our peace rather than take that of the church.

"How's your search going?" he asked one night, while we were leaning against the Monteriggioni well.

"My search for Clara, you mean? I forgot I was supposed to be searching."

"Perhaps that's the best approach."

"Maybe."

I looked around. More people were coming to the church that night, although we still had our privacy in that little spot by the well. I took some time to think whether I should tell him or not, after all, nothing was yet finished. But then I told him that I was writing music that I might play with my roommates.

"You are composing jazz to play with the guys?"

"Yes. Right now I'm working on one called *The Story You Don't Know*. It was inspired by you and William, your photos, your stories, and our dances. I hope it has the same warmth and vibe."

"Ah, I'm so happy. I must hear it."

"Well, it might take a while to complete. I hope soon. It feels so good to be creating something. I love writing music and playing it, imagining the dialogue among the instruments. And the guys are fantastic."

"Sounds wonderful."

"I have the feeling that this is something I was meant to do. It's like breathing again. It's like breathing."

"Yes," he smiled, "like breathing."

"Will you perform?"

"Yes. We're working on a set. We'd like to play at the *Umbria Jazz Festival*, perhaps this July."

"The one we went to? The one in Perugia?"

"Yes."

28

And so Andrea, Paolo, Renato, and I worked on making that dream come true.

We spent more and more hours practicing the pieces I had sketched for us. *The Story You Don't Know, Looking for Clara, What Does Love Mean, Once Upon a Night, Meeting Lady Moon, When a Seagull Fell in Love with a Raven.* Renato had also composed some pieces, and we were all working on.

That spring we played at local clubs and bars whenever we could. The audience must have enjoyed our music, as the bars and clubs kept inviting us back. Obviously, I was not making enough money to pay my bills and so, perhaps inspired by Anna's story that I had now made mine, I started teaching piano at home. I initially had two students. They were the ten-year-old twins of Lucia, my next-door neighbor, who had listened to me playing and loved my music. But then Lucia talked to the parents of the twins' schoolmates, and suddenly I had ten more students. Teaching made me feel even closer to Anna.

In April, the principal of the boys' elementary school

called me and offered me a temporary position as a music teacher. The full-time teacher was on maternity leave, and they needed someone to cover for her while she was away. And so I started doing that too.

The kids were delightful. They would come to class with their big smiles and huge backpacks that were bigger than themselves. They called me "Maestra!," each time shouting that name with so much enthusiasm and joy that I wished I could have captured that sound to re-play it every time I needed to remind myself of what joy was. They teased me because of my accent, and laughed, their laughs resonating in the big hall that led to our classroom. Ours was a music class, and at times I felt their laughs and chats were making more music than the music itself. They had a mysterious way of making everything look so simple and beautiful. Sometimes they reminded me of Mario. Their pure joy was overwhelming.

My days were filled with music and novels again, as they had been before law school. I read some of the Russian classics I hadn't yet read, Tolstoy, Dostoyevsky, and Nabokov. Mario suggested these authors to me, and we read some novels together and talked about them. His life and experiences suggested meanings and nuances I would have missed without him.

"You are an artist," I told him one day, after he had shared with me his thoughts on a passage from Tolstoy's *Kreutzer Sonata*.

"I was just lucky enough to have an artistic life."

Yes, he was. And he was an artist.

One day Andrea came home holding a piece of paper in his hand. There was a phone number on it. He said he had met with someone who had attended our show the night before and thought we should play at *Umbria Jazz* that July.

He said this guy knew some people in the organization who would be thrilled to have us there. He asked Andrea for our name and whether we had a CD, and the four of us realized that we actually needed both.

We talked about various possibilities for the name of our group, English and Italian options, and I finally came up with an idea.

"What about calling us "*Quartetto Bassi*?"

I'm not sure why I suggested that name. Perhaps it reminded me of the search, the art, the journey. The guys liked it, especially when I explained to them where it came from. And so that became our name.

We needed a CD. We had two months to record one, and our set list included more than enough original material. We all agreed without much discussion that the title of the CD would be *The Story You Don't Know.* And we registered for the *Umbria Jazz Festival* as the *Quartetto Bassi*, with *The Story You Don't Know.*

Andrea found a recording studio in Siena that offered us a special deal. Mario took the photos for our album and we decided to use the Monteriggioni church for the cover.

We practiced obsessively, met for our recording sessions every day at 3 p.m., and recorded until late at night. When we finished recording and could hold the CD in our hands, it was hard to believe that was actually happening and we would be playing in Perugia the next month. And then we got the assigned location and time. Another surprise. We would play at the *Giardini Carducci*, at 8 p.m. Right where Joe had played the year before.

When I met with Mario for dinner that night, and I showed him the CD and the invitation letter from the jazz festival, he looked at me, raised his eyebrows, and smiled.

"Interesting," he said. "The circle is about to close."

I didn't understand exactly what he meant by that, but I was distracted and too anxious about the performance to think about anything other than the concert.

"Who else is playing there?" he asked.

"I have no idea."

"There must be a program, no? The festival starts in less than ten days."

He was right. I should have checked. But perhaps I hadn't because I didn't want to discover that big names were playing right before or after us, or that some other name was on that list.

"Is Joe performing?"

I knew he was going to ask that.

"I don't know."

"Aren't you curious?"

I looked down, and didn't respond. Instead I asked Mario if he would come with us. He had come to most of our performances in Siena, but each time he had seemed more tired, and perhaps now a trip to Perugia might be too much. That year, Mario would turn ninety.

"We could go by car," I said, trying to show him that this trip might be more comfortable than the other one we had done together.

He lowered his head and I noticed that his eyebrows and hair had all turned white. When did that happen?

"I think you will need to do that by yourself, Clara. I would love to be there when you play. Who could have said last year that only a year later you would be playing at the *Giardini*. With your band. And your own music. I really wish I could come, but perhaps another time. Who knows?"

That reaction seemed unusual for him, but he was getting older, and maybe that was his way of showing me what I refused to see.

After dinner, he asked me if I would walk him home and so I did. He took my hand and didn't let go until we were in front of his building. His touch was warmer than usual, and seemed to be talking to me about our friendship and our past together.

"Clara, enjoy the moment, and don't think about anything else. It's not about the performance, remember. It's about the journey, the one you made to get here. And shouldn't you be proud already?"

Yes, I was.

"The last years had been particularly hard for me," he said. "But then we met, and you reminded me that life is worth living until the last breath."

He paused, and then said,

"I've a favor to ask. Would you finish working on my stories?"

I promised him I would, he kissed my forehead, entered his building, and his deep, full laugh resonated in the hall.

I smiled, and as I walked back home, I thought I should bring Mario's laugh with me to Perugia. And so I did.

29

We didn't have enough money to stay for the entire festival, so we agreed to stay for just one night. We rented a van and drove to Perugia while listening to our CD and making predictions on our performance. Some silly ones, and some more serious ones. Renato asked Andrea to check the schedule to see who would be playing before and after us, and when he read Joe's name on that list, my heart stopped beating.

So perhaps this was what Mario meant when he said that the circle was about to close. He had seen that circle closing before I had. Although I should have known, as I had drawn and walked along circles like that one often. My music. William. And now Joe. Hard to predict how would this one close.

It seemed like yesterday, but a year had passed. And while I'd spent my time playing and trying to get back to my music, while I'd been composing and playing in clubs and making new friends, while I'd discovered that the mother I had never met died, Joe had lived his own life, and I had no idea how that was.

Perugia looked the same as the year before, except that Mario wasn't there, and I felt his absence. I took the same walk we took together, went to the same street where I had met Joe, and passed by *La Bottega*, where Joe and I were supposed to meet and never did. That corner of Perugia seemed completely different now. It was crowded and noisy, and I felt lighter and more at peace with myself. Happy.

I stayed there for a while, thinking of the journey I had made to return to that very same place. I thought about my music and rehearsed it in my head. All that mattered to me now was my music, and our concert. When I returned to the hotel, I took a shower and sat for a while on the balcony of my room. The air was warm, I felt relaxed, and almost fell asleep. Then Andrea called and it was time to go.

"Clara Bassi and her quartet," said the host, and I thought that was hilarious. We all smiled, excited and ready to perform. As we walked to the stage, up on the same stairs where Joe and I had last seen each other, I looked down and I saw Joe. At that point, I was not surprised at all. He was in the audience, and our eyes met. He looked exactly the same, his beard perhaps a bit longer. But while I was not surprised, he was in complete disbelief. They had my name as Clara Bassi on the program.

The audience applauded and it pulled me back to my music, the one I had written, the one I wanted to share.

I took a deep breath, seated myself at the piano, and waited for Andrea to start beating the time. And then everything disappeared. The host, the guys, Joe. I was back in Brussels. I felt a rush of fear in my chest. Then an immediate warmth. But then I thought about Mario's laugh and his words, and they reminded me that, after all, I was there to have fun. The announcer seemed a bit unsure of what our first number would be. Renato, who was close to him, took the initiative and whispered the name in his ear. But the man turned the microphone to Renato, and everyone heard him say "*The Story You Don't Know*." The audience laughed, we all laughed, Andrea beat the time, and we started.

Our music was full and loud. I felt each measure, our chemistry, Renato's improvisations, mine, Paolo's arrangements. I was part of it, and it felt natural. I was there. My story was there. Not hiding myself anymore. The audience liked our music and we saw people dancing and moving with it.

We then played *Meeting Lady Moon*, *Once Upon a Night*, and we ended with *What Does Love Mean*. It was a success and when we were done, I looked at the audience and for a moment I thought I saw Mario.

I was the last to leave the stage, and as I hurried down the stairs to join the rest of the group, I ran into Joe.

"You were wonderful," he said. "I didn't know you were still in Italy and that you were such a great pianist."

As I heard him talk, I felt as if I were meeting him for the first time.

"I think we should talk, don't you?" he then asked.

I wanted to talk to him, but now felt a sting of resentment.

"Will you send me to another restaurant and make me wait until the sun rises?"

"I'm sorry," he said. "That should have not happened. And it won't happen again. I promise."

I looked for the guys. Renato was looking at me trying to understand what was happening. I had never mentioned Joe to them so he could not know.

"I have to think about it," I said.

"Clara, please."

He was right. We needed to talk.

"O.K., but then come to my hotel." I gave him the address, and we agreed to meet in the lobby at around midnight.

Renato asked me about Joe and I told them the story. But we mainly talked about the concert, as at that point, for some reason, that felt like the most important thing to me.

Andrea suggested we go to a *taverna*, sort of a pub, close to our hotel, and we had dinner there. At about midnight, when we returned to the hotel, Joe was in the lobby waiting for me.

I introduced him to the guys, they shook hands and he complimented them for their performance. They exchanged a few comments on the pieces, and then we said goodbye and went for a walk.

30

We walked to a bench on a hill that overlooked the city. It was past midnight but we could still hear the music coming from a concert somewhere nearby.

"How've you been?" he asked.

I smiled.

"That's a hard question to start with. Try again."

"How are you now?"

"Better. Much better"

"I know you left your job," he said.

"Yes, I did. A year ago."

"Adam said they thought something serious had happened to you and you needed to take a break."

"Right," I said, but didn't say more. I wanted to hear his questions, and soon he asked them.

"What happened? Why did you disappear? Not an email, a call? You have no idea what you did to me."

"I'm sorry," I said. "I needed time to understand."

"And now? Do you know?"

"When I met you I didn't know I could feel the way I did.

Ever. I had never felt anything like that before, and I didn't know it could happen so fast. I thought my feelings could not be real. That they ought to be the product of fantasy, fear, confusion. And so I ran away."

I didn't know what more to say. I thought about the music I had composed. I thought it could have answered his questions, and mine. Words could never express what I was feeling. Or at least I felt so.

He remained silent, staring at the city lights that seemed so far away. Everything looked so peaceful. That peace overwhelmed me. I closed my eyes and let it do that.

"I discovered that my mother died when I was born," I then said. "She was Italian. The woman who has been my mother for the past twenty-nine years was not my birth mother."

"When did you find out?" he asked, looking sorry for me, and perhaps sorry for not having looked for me before.

"Just before I quit my job."

"How did you find out?"

"My father decided to tell me the truth."

"I see," he said, and then remained silent for a while.

"What about you? Are you...?" He did not let me finish my question.

"At some point," he said, "I concluded that I had imagined us. It took me some time to get over you, but then I...I married Sarah. She's pregnant."

I suddenly felt cold and wanted to leave.

"That's awesome. I'm happy for you." I gazed over the roof of the houses, the scattered, bright lights and the alleys. So it was over. Now what?

I looked at my diary, the one where I had been writing letters to him almost every day since I had left L.A., and felt I needed to get rid of it.

"I think this belongs to you," I said, and handed it to him.

"What is it?"

"Something I wrote but don't want to keep. Maybe you won't like to keep it either. You could just skim it and trash it. Read it and trash it. Or just trash it."

I paused and then said,

"It's getting cold." I stood up and started walking back to the hotel.

"Clara, wait. Did you love me?"

I turned, smiled, and said,

"I think I could have."

31

When I got to the hotel, the guys were gathered in the lobby. Their faces were dark. They had received a phone call from Siena. Mario had died. He had a respiratory arrest while walking on a street. He was taken to the hospital but it was too late. The doctor said he had not suffered and that it was quick.

We drove back to Siena that night and arrived in the early morning. I ran to Mario's apartment. Several of his friends were there. A priest was making the sign of the cross with his fingers on his forehead. I had never seen anyone dead before, and I refused to look at him. I knew he wasn't there anymore.

I looked around his room trying to find him somewhere. At some point I heard him laugh softly from a distance.

"Clara," an old man called me to a corner of the room.

"Mario wanted you to have this," he said, and pointed to the footlocker. On top of it, there was a folder with a light-green cover, and the words "*Finding Clara*," in a thick, black stroke. I opened the file and found the photo Mario had taken of me the day we first met in *Piazza del Campo* and a story he had written for me. I took that file and the foot-locker with me, and went back to my apartment.

Mario had died. Siena had disappeared, and everything looked meaningless and empty. The next week, I returned the piano to the company from which I had rented it, collected my things, packed, and prepared to leave.

The day before my flight, as I was making coffee, someone knocked on the door. I waited for the guys to answer but then realized I was the only one left in the apartment. It was almost noon. I had stayed up all night and probably fell asleep only after sunrise. I searched for my pants, pulled them on, and went to the door to answer.

I looked through the peephole, and saw an older woman who looked familiar. I squeezed my eyes wondering whether I was dreaming. That couldn't be true. Was Clara standing in front of my door? Was it really her?

I opened the door and did not say a word.

"*Buongiorno. Sono Clara Bassi. Un'amica di Mario. La disturbo*?"

My legs were shaking for the lack of sleep and food and, even after she spoke, I still thought I could be dreaming.

"*No certo, entri pure per favore.*"

I watched her as she entered the apartment with elegance and grace. An older version of myself, almost a vision. She looked at me and smiled.

"*Mamma mia, davvero sembra di rivedermi trent'anni fa. Che emozione!*" She noticed our resemblance and seemed moved by it.

I asked her how she found me. She explained that Mario had found her and contacted her, and that she and Mario were planning to surprise me. They were supposed to meet the day before in front of *Bar Termini*, the old *Café Siena*. But when she got there, she saw the poster announcing his death. She had his and my address, and so she first went to Mario's place and when she found it deserted, she came looking for me.

I felt disoriented. Mario's death and that meeting. I tried to explain to her how I felt and she seemed to understand. I said I didn't feel like talking, so she took my hand and told me her story.

She had left Siena after she fell in love with a man she had met on a train to Perugia. His name was Klaus. He was from Nuremberg. When the two married, she moved to Germany with him. She missed Marta and Verde and her life in Siena, but she thought that the only way for her to be comfortable with her new life was to leave the past behind.

Her life in Germany had been the normal life of a wife and a mother. She had three children and now had five grandchildren, one of which, Elisa, was just learning to play piano.

I asked her whether she still played or taught piano. She did not. Occasionally, she would sit close to Elisa, though, and help her on this or that piece. She said she was still baking, although she no longer had a bakery. The only bakery she ever owned was *Café Siena*.

I told her I had just made coffee and asked her if she would share it with me. She nodded and, as I poured the coffee in the cups, she came to the kitchen and noticed my *torta di mele*, the one I had made before leaving for Perugia. She examined it, put her nose closer to it to test its aroma, and then asked me where I bought it. I told her I had made it several days ago and she should not try it.

"*L'hai fatta prima della morte di Mario, vero*?"

Yes, I had made it before Mario's death and I wasn't

interested in that any more. In fact, no one in the house was. She came closer to me and hugged me.

We sat on the sofa. She noticed I could barely hold my cup in my hands and put hers around mine to help me sustain it.

"*Raccontami di Mario e della vostra amicizia, vuoi?*" she then asked.

I told her about Mario, how we met, the journey that her photo had triggered, my desire to find her. I told her about our trip to Roma and our meeting with Verde, our trip to Sorrento, and our meeting with Marta. She asked detailed questions about them and told me she and Mario had also planned to surprise them. Now she would go visit them by herself. That circle was about to close too, but Mario would not be part of it.

I told Clara how much she meant to Mario, how he had described her in the story. She asked me if she could read it.

I said I would, and as I read Mario's story for her, she closed her eyes, somehow trying to go back to the times and events in that story. Was everything in that story accurate? I wanted to ask her, but then decided not to. After all, all that had happened up to that moment could be described as a dream, one with happy and sad moments. And dreams are never accurate. Or perhaps they are, sometimes more than reality itself. It just depends on us and the way we read them.

I looked at her as I was reading to check her expressions from time to time, and see if she had questions. She seemed to have accepted life, she seemed to have known and experienced love, and she looked way more confident than the woman in the photograph and the one in Mario's story. I wondered if I would ever be where she seemed to be.

After I finished reading, she said the story was accurate

and that she did not know Mario was such a careful reader of people. And she did not remember sharing all those personal, intimate details with him. He must have gathered some of them from her conversations with friends and customers. However, obviously the ending was not accurate. I explained to her that Mario felt uncomfortable leaving her story without an ending, and that he felt compelled to create one.

We talked about why she had trouble playing in public and she said that she was too lazy to face the audience. She thought every artist, or almost every artist has trouble facing the audience, but then if the artist loves her art, she will learn how to overcome that fear. I thought she was right.

I asked her what she thought about love. She said love was responsible for all her choices in life and she did not regret a single one. She said she was relatively older when she fell in love. Perhaps that had helped.

"*Perchè mi cercavi?*" she then asked.

I told her I thought she might give me the answers I was looking for. I explained that we seemed to share so much. Our music, our mutual fear to play in public, our passion for art, baking, and so I thought she might know better than I did who I was and what I could become. She smiled and confessed that she had many questions that had no answer, but said this was what she liked the most. The continuous search for answers, the journeys, and the many things left to unfold. She was probably right.

After a while, she checked the time and told me she had a bus to catch soon. She asked me if I would take a walk with her. We walked to *Via Termini* so she could take a final look at what had been her *Caffé*. Yes, the table and the chairs were the same.

"*E' un cuore o un cappello*?" she asked me, pointing to the back of the chair. I said it could be either of the two depending on your mood and what you wanted to see in there. She smiled, hugged me, and said goodbye.

I watched her walk along *Via Termini* back to the bus stop. It was precisely how I had imagined her once.

32

That night I returned to Monteriggioni. I felt I had not properly said goodbye to Mario and there were many things I wanted to ask him. I needed to silence the noise, to make that telescope that would let me see him, touch his hands again.

I thought about going there by taxi, but I remembered the unique experience of our journey together that night, on the bus, the first time we went there, and so I took the bus instead.

I sat in the back, as he loved to do and as we had done that night. A lady asked me if she could sit close to me and, without thinking about it, I replied that she could not, as a friend was going to join me soon.

That seat, unfortunately, remained empty, and most likely that lady thought I was crazy. I felt disoriented.

The route to Monteriggioni was almost deserted and the bus made only a few stops along the way.

I thought of the events that had troubled me so much in the past, when I thought William had betrayed me, when I discovered my feelings for Joe, when I had to let him go before leaving for Italy, the time I found and lost my mother, and when Joe told me he had married Sarah and they were having a baby. Mario's death was not comparable to any of them. He was gone. A harsh punch in my stomach that had left me breathless. I had stopped breathing and had just started filtering in a few molecules of oxygen to survive day-to-day. I felt like in a coma, my condition known to myself only. At times I felt I wanted to scream and cry, but I had no energy, no voice, no sound to make.

And so, still in my coma, I arrived in Monteriggioni.

The town looked exactly as I had seen it the first time. Still, everything else had changed. I had changed. I looked at the well in the square in front of the church, and I thought I saw Mario and me leaning against it and laughing. That would not happen again. Never again.

"Mario, this is so unfair," I cried.

And then I felt like something was dragging me inside the church. I felt as if someone was holding my hand and pulling me inside. There were two people sitting in the pew closest to the altar. I sat in the back. Would they hear me?

"Mario, where are you?" I whispered, but nobody answered.

"Are you there? Can you hear me?"

Still no answer.

"I feel awful, and I don't know what to do. I feel I'm running away from Siena, running away from the guys and from everything that made me happy, but you're no longer here and I can't stay. I can't go to *Piazza del Campo*. That would remind me of the time we met. And I can't walk on *Banchi di Sopra*, as I would look up to your balcony and think about our time in your living room, dancing on the jazz notes and laughing. I simply can't, Mario. Hey, can you hear me?"

I must have actually spoken that last sentence aloud, as a priest came closer to me.

"*C'è qualcosa che non va? Vuoi fare una chiaccherata*?" he asked.

No, I did not want to talk to a stranger. I did not want to talk to a priest.

"I'm not Catholic," I said, trying to push him away.

He smiled and said it was O.K., that that did not matter, that we could talk. He said he heard my prayer and he wanted to help. How is that he had heard my prayer? Wasn't I silent? I wanted to resist, push him away, but I still felt like I was under anesthesia, too weak to react, too weak to ask questions. So I let him sit close to me.

He asked me how I felt and why I was crying.

Was I? Again? I had not noticed.

I remained silent, looking at him, and then without even realizing I was doing so, I started talking. Or perhaps I was sleeptalking.

I told him about Mario and our relationship. I must have talked for a long time. He just listened, held my hand, and then said something that reminded me of Mario, of something he had said to me. The priest said that love comes with pain, and if I was feeling pain that meant I had loved. It meant I had loved my friend. Wasn't that beautiful?

He asked me whether, if I had been offered an opportunity to go back, change the course of the events so that I would never meet him, I would prefer that. Obviously not, I said.

"*Perchè no*?" he asked.

Mario had been one of the most beautiful things that had happened to me. He had made me feel happy and fulfilled. And so, no, how could I prefer that I had never met him?

He smiled and asked me to think about that when I felt that the pain was unbearable. He said I had to have faith, that life could be hard, but then beautiful again. It was just a matter of time. And the more darkness I was experiencing, the more light would be awaiting me.

His words, his way of talking had brought Mario back to me. Did he know Mario?

As I left the church, I heard Mario laugh.

I left the next day for Los Angeles. William was getting married and I promised him I'd be there.

Saying goodbye to the guys wasn't easy. They were worried about me but understood my need to leave. They said they would wait for me, as they were sure I would return. I wasn't.

My flight arrived in L.A. at night. I took a taxi to my apartment. It was exactly as I had left it. So hard to believe it was over a year and a half ago.

I was home and I had found Clara, I had found myself, but Mario had died, and I had just lost a big part of me with him.

I lay my suitcase on the floor and I was back in time again. My memories were too loud and so I left the apartment, hoping they would not follow me.

An old, disheveled lady was giving away cats. She had several in small cages. I stopped to look at them. She explained that the two I was looking at were siblings and she preferred that they be adopted together. I felt lonely and thought they could be my new friends, in my new life. And so I took them home with me.

When I returned to my place with my cats, I sat on my sofa, and pulled *Finding Clara*, the story Mario had written for me.

I missed Mario immensely. He would know exactly what

to say and do to make me feel better, to make life magic again.

I looked around and didn't see much. Just the recall file I should have worked on, my graduation ring, my damaged Prada shoe. None of this belonged to me anymore, but perhaps it never did.

I walked to the stereo, put *The Story You Don't Know* on, and fell asleep.

I woke up at sunrise.

I felt the same emptiness I had felt the night before and the nights before that. I lay there for hours, unable to move and start that new day. Finally, I got up and went to the kitchen. I looked at my Prada shoe and the ring again. I searched the house and found the other shoe. What an accomplishment, I thought. Now I could get rid of them. I put on my jeans, my sneakers, and went out looking for someone to give them to.

The cat lady was in the same spot where I had met her the night before.

"Hey, would you like these?"

She looked at the box with the shoes and the ring.

"Is this for real? These look expensive," she said.

"Yes, it's for real."

I handed her the box as she kept staring at me.

On the way back home I went to the café I used to stop at. The lady who had always made my coffee was no longer there, but one of the girls I had seen the last time I had been there was still sitting on the sofa where I had seen her that day. This time, a guy was close to her, holding her hand.

I smiled, paid for my coffee, and walked home.

Once there, I grabbed the light-green file with my name on it and started reading my story. The first line read:

Love comes from pain but love is the only thing that matters. Thirty years later, I found Clara and she reminded me of that.

That was my story, our story. Slowly, the emptiness faded away.

THE END

ACKNOWLEDGMENTS

Looking for Clara was born out of a dream, on a summer night, so I'd like to thank that dream that woke me up with a strong desire of looking beyond a line, an idea.

But above all, I want thank Aaron, the love of my life, for pushing me to write this story and helping me in every step of the way.

And I want to thank Allan, my best friend and mentor, for reading so many versions of my story with love and dedication and support, always, no matter what, for his superb editing, for his questions, for pushing me, for making me succeed and turn my *Clara* dream into reality.

Clara would have never been possible without the two of them.

And then thank you, Friends, for reading, for loving *Clara*, for asking me for more and pushing me to write the sequel, which is indeed forthcoming. Thank-you! My book launch events would have probably been empty rooms when I started if I didn't have all of you right there with me, to cheer for and support me. I wanted to write Clara to share with you all the love that I had inside of me.

So thank you friends and readers for letting me do it.

simona

DID YOU LIKE THIS BOOK?

If you enjoyed this book, I'd be so thankful if you could leave an honest review online. You can post your review on Amazon, Barnes & Noble, Goodreads or any other bookstore that you like.

Thank you for your support!

simona

GET A FREE COPY OF LIKE STILL WATER

Building a relationship with my readers is the very best thing about writing. I occasionally send newsletters with details on new releases, special offers and other bits of news related to the characters I create.

And if you sign up to the mailing list, I'll send you a free copy of *Looking for Clara*'s prequel: *Like Still Water.*

You can get your free copy by signing up here:

http://simonawrites.com/gift

ABOUT THE AUTHOR

Simona Grossi was born and raised in a small town in Italy, surrounded by books and music. She studied piano for several years, then became a lawyer, a teacher, a writer. She considers art as a form of love and love as a form of art.

ALSO BY SIMONA GROSSI

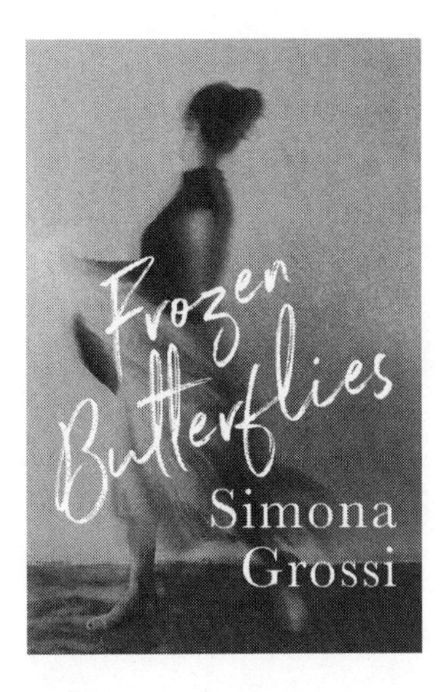

FROZEN BUTTERFLIES: A NOVEL

The night is her closest companion. But some truths can only be found in the harsh light of day...

Susan is tormented by her hidden history. Driven by dark thoughts and sleepless nights, she forges a bond with a blogger who has troubles of his own. But when they discover a compelling, mysterious journal, sharing the excerpts with the world unleashes a dangerous attraction...

Made in the USA
Columbia, SC
14 February 2020